# LOVE SET APART

## BOOK ONE OF EDNA'S WORLD

JENNAE VALE

# PROLOGUE



Emilie Toussaint held the rose-colored stone close to her heart as she gazed at the now full moon. She sat on the banks of the river Seine with little care for the beautiful gown she wore. What did it matter if it was soiled by the mud or water? Her life was about to change in ways that caused her much sadness and had led her to this place. It was her last and only hope.

A week ago, she had been told of a woman who could possibly help her with a potion or some other token that would change her fate. So she made her way from the palace she called home toward a place she'd never been allowed to venture in the past. She was apprehensive, but her heartache urged her forward through the darkened streets of Paris to the ramshackle home of Madame DuBois. She knocked and in only a moment was told to enter.

Despite its outward appearance, the interior of the small cottage was neat and clean. Pots and vials were neatly arranged on shelves, and fresh flowers and herbs were displayed in so many cups and vases that Emilie assumed there were none left for any other use.

"Good evening, Mademoiselle." Madame Dubois emerged from behind a particularly large floral bouquet. She was short and stout, with a soft round face that seemed kind.

"Good evening." A hesitant smile appeared on Emilie's lips.

"Do not be afraid, my dear. I will not harm you. My intention is only to do good." She eyed Emilie with a soft twinkle in her eyes. "Especially for those who seek me out. How can I be of service?"

"I was told you could help me with a problem." Emilie nervously glanced around the room.

"Here. Sit." Madame Dubois motioned to a chair placed by a small round table then sat across from Emilie. "Now, I cannot help you if you don't tell me everything."

Emilie drew in a deep breath, blowing it out and doing her best to relax before she began to speak. "There is a man I am to marry. His name is Comte Matteo Barbieri." She hesitated, wondering if she was making a mistake. Was it even possible that this woman would be able to help her? Emilie had never believed in witches or magic, but it seemed this was the only choice left to her.

"And you do not wish to marry him?"

Emilie cleared her throat and straightened in her chair. A warm glow from a fire in the hearth filled the room. "No. My father has arranged the marriage. And the man is much older than I."

Madame Dubois nodded her head in understanding.

"I am in love with another. Robert MacMillan has declared his love for me, but we both know that a marriage is impossible for us because he is a soldier without a title. He is... not suitable for me." The words were bitter in her mouth. Robert was the best man she had ever met. She folded her hands in front of her on the tabletop and did her best not to fidget. "I don't know what to do. That is why I am here."

"Nothing is impossible." Madame DuBois' voice was loud and strong, causing Emilie to flinch. Seeming to realize she might be frightening Emilie, she took on a softer tone. "How long have you known this Robert?" Madame DuBois arose, retrieved two cups and placed one in front of Emilie before pouring them both something unrecognizable from a ceramic ewer.

"What is this?" Emilie asked looking into the murky liquid in front of her.

"A delicious drink that I make," Madame Dubois proudly stated. "It will help you relax." She held up her cup. "I will drink first so you know it will not harm you." The cup was drained and placed on the table. "Now you." Madame DuBois motioned with her hand for Emilie to lift her cup.

Emilie did as directed, lifting the cup to her lips all the while expecting something bitter and undrinkable. Pleasantly surprised at the sweet lemony liquid she tasted, Emilie also drained her cup. "Thank you. It was quite good."

"Yes. I know. Now where were we?" She tapped her chin, then tipped her head as she gazed at Emilie. "We were speaking of Robert."

Emilie was hesitant. She wasn't used to speaking to strangers, but in order to get the help she needed, she would have to trust Madame DuBois. She closed her eyes, blowing out the breath she'd been holding. "I've known him for a year now. He came to Paris to guard the young king."

"You met him at the palace?"

"I am a member of the court. A lady-in-waiting to Marie de Medici."

"I see." If Madame DuBois was surprised by this information, she kept it hidden. "Does she know how you feel about Robert?"

"She does, but she agrees with my father that I should not marry below my station. In fact, she helped arrange the marriage. The Comte is from Italy and a family friend of the Queen Mother's."

Madame DuBois' eyes opened wide with surprise. "That certainly complicates matters, doesn't it?"

The effects of the drink were becoming apparent to Emilie. She was no longer nervous and felt quite comfortable speaking with Madame DuBois. "I cannot marry him."

A sympathetic nod of her head was followed by a sad smile. "We can do anything, if we must."

Emilie's heart sank. She wasn't going to get her help here.

"Do not look so forlorn. Just because you can does not mean you will." She chuckled softly as she patted Emilie's hand. "Now, first I must be sure you truly love Robert."

"Oh, I do. I love him so much." Her heart felt as though it might burst from her chest as she spoke the words. She'd never felt this way before. Robert was all she thought about from morning to night.

"You would not mind being the wife of a soldier? It's not easy you know." Madame DuBois tipped her head and examined Emilie's face, perhaps for any sign that she would waver in her resolve.

"I would not mind at all. I do not enjoy life at court." She wrinkled her nose at the thought of it.

"Well, then I will do my best to help you. You deserve happiness and since you have risked so much to come to me, I will aid you in your quest for love. There are no guarantees it will work. Much is up to you."

"I'll do anything." Emilie clasped her hands in a prayerlike gesture. Excitement bubbled inside of her as she leaned forward in her chair ready for her instructions.

Madame DuBois rose once again. This time she went to the shelves filled with bottles and vials. Emilie watched her every move and was surprised when she returned with something other than a bottle. In her hand was a rose-colored stone unlike anything Emilie had ever seen before. Placing the stone in her palm, Emilie examined it. The translucence was intriguing to the eye. There was a softness to it despite its rough edges, and the color was the most beautiful shade of pale pink. She glanced up to see Madame DuBois smiling proudly at her. "What am I to do with it?"

"I'll tell you." Madame DuBois took Emilie's hand in hers, encouraging her to wrap her fingers around the stone. "On the night of the next full moon, in seven days, you must take this stone to the river. There you should hold the stone close to your heart and tell the moon what you want. Do not be vague in your speech. Tell the moon of your love and your wishes."

"The moon will hear me?"

"Of course. Say your wishes out loud and then toss the stone into the river. I have already cast a spell on the stone, it will strengthen your words as you speak them. When you have finished, you must thank the moon. That part is very important."

"That is all I need to do?" Emilie was feeling a little skeptical of these instructions.

"Yes."

"And Robert and I will be able to marry?"

"The moon will hear you. I cannot guarantee marriage, but you will receive the help you need to find happiness."

Emilie looked down at the stone in her hand. It seemed to sparkle and shine more as she gazed on it. "Thank you." She reached into her cloak and from a hidden pocket removed a pouch of coins for Madame DuBois.

"Thank you, Mademoiselle. You must tell no one where you've been. You understand that it would be dangerous for me."

"I won't tell anyone. I promise."

"I have placed a spell of protection on you, so you may walk back to the palace in safety. Go and be well."

The week had gone by slower than Emilie could possibly have imagined and the date of her upcoming nuptials to Comte Barbieri loomed in the future. She hadn't seen Robert since she had spoken to Madame DuBois. He'd been away traveling with the king and Emilie wondered if she'd ever see him again. She gazed up at the moon as she cradled the stone next to her heart and spoke the words she'd rehearsed over and over again in her head. This was her one and only chance to change what was about to occur.

"Oh, beautiful moon, I am Emilie Toussaint, daughter of Comte Toussaint. I come to you for help. I am in love with Robert MacMillan and I wish to marry him. Will you please help me? I am sure that you can." Even as she said the words, she doubted them. She remembered what Madame DuBois had told her. That she must be sure of her words and so she repeated them again, this time without doubts and with more strength in her voice, and when she was done she thanked the moon and tossed her offering of the rose stone into the river. It plopped without incident into the dark depths of the flowing water.

She'd done it and now she would wait for whatever was to come her way.

CHAPTER

# ONE

What had once been a dark and eerie close leading to the offices of The Council of Witches was now filled with color. Window boxes filled with flowers adorned the once drab brick walls. Edna Campbell had seen to that herself. Why should the only access to the council offices be so foreboding that it frightened potential clients away before they even had a chance to meet with the witches? Yes, the sun seemed to shine brighter and the narrow path appeared wider as she made her daily trek from her flat to her new job with The Council of Witches.

Edna straightened her wrap and brushed a single strand of blue hair from her face as she hummed softly to herself. She was quite pleased with her recent accomplishments here in Edinburgh. Aside from the close, she'd also done some work in the actual office itself. The other three witches, while very good at what they did, were anything but organized. The offices had been just as drab as the close had been. Edna saw to an immediate redo of everything. The walls were painted in light, bright colors and overhead lighting presented a warm welcome to visitors. The decor was updated, but also paid homage to those who had come before them, with portraits of witches past and present lining the hallways. Work spaces, desks and other necessities reflected the unique character and quirkiness of each witch.

On the home front, she and Angus had settled into a quaint little flat right around the corner. They occupied the first and second floor of an older brick building that had probably been in existence since the 1700s. The first floor was dedicated to a small, modern kitchen and a lovely living area with a beautiful fireplace. Edna had to have a fireplace. It was how she communicated with all of the many couples past and present that she had united in love. She kept in touch as often as possible, especially with her niece Maggie and her husband Dylan, who'd taken over Edna's duties as keepers of the bridge and The Thistle & Hive Inn. They were expecting twins any day now and Edna couldn't be happier for them. On the second floor was a large bedroom with a seating area by the large picture window that over-looked the street below. A second fireplace kept them warm on chilly evenings. Angus was happy there, which made Edna's decision to work with the council so much easier.

"I'm happy wherever ye lead me, me love," he'd said, when she'd asked him how he felt about leaving The Thistle & Hive Inn and the town of Glendaloch. Edna considered herself a very lucky woman to have such a handsome, braw and loving man in her life. He liked to say her superpower was uniting people in love. It was her specialty.

Reaching the door to the council offices, Edna juggled the cups and bags she was carrying so she could open the door, but that task was almost impossible. Instead she focused on the doorknob and concentrated on turning it by using her powers. She tried not to use them for silly things like this, but the last thing she wanted to do was drop all the goodies she was bringing to share. The door opened right away, and as she made her way down the hallway it slammed behind her, causing her to jump and almost lose everything she'd worked so hard to protect. "I'll have to work on that," she muttered before entering the office. "Good morning, ladies! I've brought treats!"

Mardella, Melusina and Daire all hopped up from their seats and converged on her, each taking a cup of tea and a warm scone.

"Thank ye, Edna. I was just saying to the others how hungry I was this morning." Mardella took a bite out of her scone and rolled her eyes in obvious pleasure. "Delicious!"

"Then I arrived right in time," Edna said, removing her wrap and draping it over her chair before making herself comfortable at her desk.

"Edna yer delicious morning treats are a delight. They're like sunshine on a cloudy day," Melusina said.

Mardella and Daire groaned at the overused saying.

Melusina didn't seem to take offense though. "These scones really are delicious."

"Thank ye, Melusina. They are me signature bake," Edna said. "When I ran the inn in Glendaloch, I sold out of them every morning. I had to start making extra so nae one would be disappointed."

"We're certainly no' disappointed," Mardella said. "I could eat another if ye've brought more."

Edna reached into her tote, pulled out a container and placed it on her desk. "There are plenty here."

"Ye dinna happen to bring some butter and honey this morning, did ye?"

Edna chuckled and pointed to the container. "I couldnae forget them."

Mardella stood and helped herself to another scone, slathering it with butter and honey.

"Edna, I've news for ye," Daire said. The tallest of the three witches, she towered over the others giving her an air authority.

"Oh?" Edna put her scone down and dusted the crumbs from her fingers.

Mardella and Melusina stopped eating and turned in their seats to hear what Daire had to say.

"I ken ye've been wanting some excitement and I'm sure all the redecorating has been fun for ye, but the real reason we needed ye here was for yer gift." She circled around behind her desk.

"Of course," Edna said. "We've all got the gift."

"Right. However, yer gift is one of matchmaking." Daire reminded her. She picked up a paper from a pile stacked by her computer.

"I do love matching couples," Edna replied. She turned in her seat to fully face Daire. "I do have other talents though."

"I'm no' saying ye doona." Daire cleared her throat. "What I'm trying to say is that there's a situation that needs yer special skills." She eyed Edna before continuing. "Yer matchmaking skills."

Edna tipped her head, waiting for her to get to the point.

"There is a young lass in need of yer help," Melusina interrupted. She tossed her fiery red hair back over her shoulders.

"Really? Where are they?" Edna looked from one witch to the other wishing one of them would get to the point. Patience was a skill Edna was finding she had to work on, especially when dealing with her co-workers.

"She lives in the past. It will require ye traveling through time to help her," Mardella said before taking another bite out of her scone.

"Tell me more." Edna's curiosity was piqued.

"Well, it seems that she has had an issue that has set her apart from the man she loves. It is a situation that must be resolved. We received an urgent message from the lass. She's made a wish on the full moon, guided by one of our members who lives in Paris."

"If we've a member there, why do ye need me help?" Edna asked.

"She's no' as capable as ye." Melusina said, seeming frustrated at the interruption.

Edna knew she was good at what she did, but it was nice to hear a witch she admired acknowledge it. "I see. When would ye like me to leave?"

"Today. The sooner the better. Ye may bring Angus with ye. Ye may need his protection." Daire looked over the paper in her hand.

Edna was surprised and excited. Finally, a job outside of the office. She didn't think she'd need protection, but it would be nice to have Angus there with her. She hated to be separated from him. "Where and when exactly am I going?"

"Ye will be off to Paris. The year is 1614. The lad is Robert MacMillan. He is a Scottish guard to the young King Louis XIII. Louis' mother, Marie de Medici, is his regent until he comes of age." She looked up at Edna, who nodded to show she was listening. "The lass, Emilie Toussaint, is French. She is a lady-in-waiting to Marie. She is from a noble family. Her father is Comte Toussaint." Melusina stopped and turned the paper over as if looking for something else, but finding nothing she placed it back down on her desk. "Ye will learn the details once ye arrive. The goal is to make her wish of a life with Robert MacMillan come true."

"The only thing that matters to me as I work, is love. We ken she loves him, but does he love her?"

"I believe so, but they've been separated, as I said." Melusina broke a tiny piece of her scone and examined it before placing it in her mouth.

Edna gave a single nod of her head. "Then they will be together again. I'll see to it."

"We expect naething less from ye, Edna."

"Be on yer way then. Go home, get Angus and meet us back here this afternoon. We'll see that ye get where ye need to be," Daire said.

Edna left her uneaten scone and tea behind as she grabbed her wrap and hurried out the door. This was what she had been waiting for. It was the reason she'd come to Edinburgh. She was going to work her magic in a time and place she was unfamiliar with, but how hard could that be? Edna's work had almost always paired people from the past with present day matches. This would be a new challenge for her and one she was eager to take on.

"Angus! Angus!" Edna shouted as she rushed into their apartment.

"I'm right here, Edna. Nae need to yell." Angus looked up from his newspaper. Edna thought he should get a tablet, but he told her he liked the feel of a real paper in his hands.

"We're going on an adventure," she breathlessly explained.

"We are? Where to?" Angus stood and dropped the paper in a heap on his chair.

"France, in the year 1614. I doona ken how long we'll be gone for, so can ye be sure to close everything up while I gather a few items I'll need?" She looked around the room, peeking underneath and behind furniture. "William! Where are ye?"

William was the cat she'd brought with them from Glendaloch. He had helped her when she was kidnapped by another witch and in return she had given him a new home. He was her familiar and had powers of his own, one of which was hiding in plain sight whenever Edna needed him.

"There ye are." Edna said as William appeared right in front of her.

"William, Angus and I are going on an adventure. Ye will stay here. Mrs. Clyman will take care of ye."

He didn't think he needed to be taken care of and let out a yowl of protest in response.

"Doona be difficult. She's going to feed ye and clean up after ye. Doona give her a hard time, do ye hear me?" Edna bent down to look him in the eye.

If he did, he certainly didn't let her know as he leisurely licked his paw and then used it to clean behind his ear.

Edna glanced at Angus who had covered his mouth to stifle his laughter.

"Verra funny," Edna said. "Let's get going."

"Will I need to bring anything?" Angus asked.

"Yer sword will do," Edna said as she bustled about the living room. "Anything else ye need, we'll get when we arrive." She stopped in her tracks and turned to Angus, her brow furrowed with worry.

"What is it?" Angus asked.

"Do ye mind joining me? I dinna think to ask."

"Do I mind? What kind of question is that? By yer side is where I wish to be."

"Ye're sure?" Edna had assumed he would be, but double and triple checking wasn't out of the question for her.

"Verra," Angus assured her.

"All right then."

"Besides if I did no' go with ye, who'd protect ye when ye got yerself into trouble?"

"Angus, I'm perfectly capable of taking care of meself, I am a witch ye ken." Why was it that everyone thought she needed to be protected? She hadn't made it this far in life without avoiding a sticky situation or two. Edna was quite sure she could overcome almost anything if need be.

"I'm verra aware." His face beamed with a mischievous grin.

"Oh, ye," Edna laughed, as he snaked an arm around her waist and reeled her into his chest.

Angus kissed the tip of her nose. "I love ye and yer witchy ways, woman. Do no' forget it."

"And I love ye and yer Highland cheekiness. Now, as much as I'd prefer to stand here smooching with ye, we've got a job to do."

Angus removed his arm from her waist, but not before kissing her breathless.

Edna couldn't speak as she brought herself back to the task at hand and moved away on unsteady feet. Looking back, Angus wore a satisfied grin that almost undid her resolve right then and there.

Edna packed a bag of witchy essentials. She took only what she felt was necessary, including a deck of cards just in case she needed help reading the situation, a wee book of spells and a potion that could heal just about any wound or illness they may encounter. In a moment of inspiration, she paused just long enough to cast a spell on the bag that might come in handy later.

William was quite put out to be left behind and he was letting her know by showing her his backside as he walked away every time she tried to pet him. "I'll be back soon. Maybe ye can come next time." He eyed her with a slight bit more interest. "It's just that this is me first job as a member of the council and I need to concentrate all me efforts on getting it right. I'd be worrying about ye the whole time. What if I lost ye?"

He stared at her a moment appearing particularly affronted—as if *he'd* get lost—then turned his back to her once again.

"I'd be miserably unhappy and ye ken it, so stop trying to make me feel bad."

William pranced away out of the room, leaving Edna to finish packing.

"Doona think I willnae remember this lovely sendoff ye're giving me, William," Edna called after him. He knew exactly what he was doing and Edna was feeling the effects of it. Guilt, sadness and worry all together almost made her relent, but she wouldn't. Not this time.

Luckily William was well-loved by Mrs. Clyman and Edna was sure he would probably gain a few pounds by the time she returned.

"Are ye almost ready?" Angus asked, peeking his head in the door.

"Ye're in a hurry, are ye no'?" Edna asked, buckling up the one bag she was bringing along. It was small enough to sling over her shoulder or tie around her waist. It was important that it didn't get in the way and become a burden instead of being the help it was meant to be.

"I'm excited to go," Angus said.

"I can tell." She glanced around making sure she wasn't forgetting anything. "I'm ready," Edna announced.

Angus stuck his elbow out for her to take. Edna gave him a peck on the cheek before they headed downstairs.

Once at the door, Edna turned to say goodbye to William. She couldn't see him, but knew he was right where he could see and hear her. "Goodbye, me little love. Be good for Mrs. Clyman and we'll see ye soon."

# TWO

Arriving at the offices of The Council of Witches, Edna had a great deal of pride in showing Angus around the place and pointing out the changes she'd made. They were alone in the office. Edna wasn't sure where the others had gone, but assumed they'd be back quickly. They wanted her to leave today and she was more than ready to go.

"Ye saw all the flowers in the close," she said.

"I did and they are beautiful. Ye've always had a green thumb, me love."

"I've done a lot here as well." She pointed out how dark it had once been and how now everything was much brighter. "I would never have said anything to the council, but it was a bit depressing in here."

"Then ye've done what ye set out to do. It's quite cheerful," Angus said.

Edna seemed pleased that Angus appreciated her efforts. "The council were a bit skeptical at first, but once I put up some colorful artwork and brought in furniture that was no' only beautiful but functional, they were quite happy."

"Where do ye think they are?" Angus asked as he wandered around the office, peeking at the papers on each desk."

"Angus." Edna shook her head. "They could be anywhere."

"Do ye think they're watching us?"

As if in answer to his question, the witches three materialized in front of them.

Edna frowned on seeing them, while Angus stood wide-eyed and perfectly still.

"Why do ye do that?" Edna huffed. She knew the answer. They thought it was good fun to throw everyone off with their show of magic power, and in Edna's mind they knew how much she hated it.

"Just practicing in case we ever need to spy on someone," Melusina said. "I doona ken why it bothers ye so."

Edna rolled her eyes heavenward. They'd had this conversation before and no matter what Edna said, they would continue to *practice* their disappearing act.

"Come, join yer husband and stand here in the middle of the room." Daire pointed to a spot on the floor right by Angus.

"Have ye got everything ye need?" Melusina asked as she and the others circled around Edna and Angus, who stood facing each other. There was just enough room for the five of them in the small empty space surrounded by desks.

"Aye." Edna looked up at Angus to be sure he was prepared. He nodded, letting her know he was ready to go.

"Ye look the part of a noblewoman of the time," Daire said, eyeing her up and down with approval.

"It's the exact look I wanted." Edna had conjured up the appropriate attire for the time for both herself and Angus. Her dress was of the softest forest green velvet with a dark brown cape and hood. She'd removed the blue streak from her hair. It was her trademark, but it wouldn't do for the time period they were traveling to. It was now all the most brilliant shade of white.

Angus wore a kilt of the time. It was much the same as the kilt he'd been wearing on the day she first met him at the bridge. Where had the time gone? It seemed only yesterday that they'd met on the very bridge where she would transport many a twenty-first century lass back in time to meet their love.

That was Maggie's job now. She would see to the bridge and to the couples. Edna let out an impatient sigh, wishing this whole process would hurry along. She was excited to be on the way as she grasped Angus by the hands and looked up into his handsome face.

The witches three moved around them in a dance of arms and scarves, undulating as they circled. Edna wished she could just use a bridge. That was what she was familiar with, but she understood that things were different now and so she waited. Before long felt herself being lifted into the air, twisting and turning and all the while holding tight to Angus. She didn't want to lose him.

As quickly as they'd lifted off, they landed. Edna felt a bit wobbly on her feet, swaying a little as Angus put a strong arm around her to keep her from falling.

"Well, here we are," Angus said. "Are ye all right now?"

"Aye. Thank ye, love. I can stand now." Edna glanced around trying to get her bearings, but was confused as to why they'd landed where they did. They were in the close. The very same close where the Council of Witches had their offices, but none of the familiar signs or the flower-filled boxes were in sight. "I'm no' sure where we should go." It wasn't like her to be this out of her element. Edna always took pride in being in charge and in control. This time she'd had to give up that control to the council, allowing them to transport her through time.

"To France," Angus said.

Edna pondered this pronouncement and began walking out of the close. She could feel Angus following along right behind her. "I hope they at least got us to the correct time period. We'll ken more as we start our journey. First, we'll need to find a ship to take us."

"To Leith then," Angus said, taking Edna's hand and placing it in the crook of his elbow. "This way."

"Ye're verra calm," Edna noted, gazing up at her husband.

"I'm with ye. As long as we're together, there's naething to be nervous about." His quiet confidence was just what she needed.

Edna took in a deep breath to chase away her irritation with the council and force her nerves to stop jangling about. Angus was right. They had each other and together they were a fierce twosome. She held her head high and strolled proudly through the streets with Angus, her rock and her protection.

"I've no' been to France," Angus said. "I'm curious about it."

"We havenae had time to go anywhere. Between the bridge and the inn, we've been quite busy. Somehow I thought the first time we traveled to Paris, it would be in our time."

"'Tis an adventure we're on," he reminded her.

She had to agree. "That it is."

They made their way to the port and after asking several men along the docks where they might find a ship sailing to France, they were directed to one called *The Mallard* that was leaving for France that day. Once they found it, Edna turned to Angus who seemed to be having the same thought she was.

"Do ye believe it to be safe?" he asked.

"If need be, I can keep it from sinking, but it leaves a lot to be desired." She looked over the ship's sails that seemed to have been repaired numerous times. The ship's deck was worn with an occasional hole here and there.

The man in charge eyed them both as they approached him. He didn't seem inclined to allow them aboard. "This is no' a passenger ship," he said.

Edna reached into her drawstring purse and pulled out two silver coins, waving them in front of the man's face. His eyes went wide as he put out his hand and once the coins were deposited there, moved aside so they could access the gangplank. "Welcome aboard!"

"How many do ye have?" Angus whispered in her ear referring to the coins.

"A never-ending supply." Edna beamed a huge grin. She was feeling more and more relaxed. She could do this. She could do anything, just as she'd conjured the coins in her purse. Her witchy ways, as Angus called them, would serve them well.

"How long will the journey be?" Edna casually asked the man.

"More 'n a month." He said, walking away.

"That cannae be." Edna turned to Angus. "We're going to have to find another way. We doona have a month to spare."

"We cannae swim," Angus said.

"Nae. Of course no'." She glanced around not sure what she was searching for.

"Is there a bridge nearby?" Angus took a look around.

"Angus, ye're a genius. There's got to be one nearby. Let's go." She grabbed his hand and they hurried off the ship and away from the pier.

"Where are ye going?" the man yelled. "We're shoving off. I'll no' give yer money back."

"Keep it," Edna called back over her shoulder. "Now to find a bridge. I doona imagine we'll find familiar ones. Me best guess is there'll be one across the Firth of Forth."

"To the Firth then," Angus said.

They hurriedly made their way through the crowded streets of Edinburgh, dodging the throngs of people everywhere and the occasional shout of "gardyloo" followed by the contents of a chamber pot being emptied from an upper window.

"Oh, my!" Edna said after a particularly close call. She stepped gingerly around the mess and practically broke into a run.

"We've got to find a carriage, love. Be on the alert." Angus lifted her off the ground and over a large puddle.

"There's one," Edna said, pointing ahead of them.

The carriage belonged to a gentleman who was now standing beside it and eyeing a building. "I'll be back shortly."

"Sir." His driver acknowledged him.

"Excuse me," Angus said, catching the man's attention. "Me wife and I wondered if we could pay ye to have yer man take us to the Firth."

"That's some distance," the man said.

"Exactly why we need yer help."

"Yer name, sir?" The man was looking them both up and down, which was understandable. How did he know they were trustworthy?

"I'm Angus Campbell and this is me wife Edna. Our driver went in search of water for the horses and has vanished with our carriage. I'd be happy to make it worth yer while."

"How worth me while?" the man asked.

"Verra." Edna reached into her pouch and took out a handful of coins along with a dose of magic that would make the man more amenable to their request.

"Verra well then." He turned to his man. "Return as soon as ye can."

Edna poked Angus in the side with her elbow, winking once as he glanced down at her. "Shall we?"

He opened the carriage door and followed her in. They sat comfortably next to each other as the driver carefully wound his way through the streets of Edinburgh and onto the road that would lead them to the Firth.

The trip took longer than either of them had anticipated. Edna fidgeted with the bag she'd brought along, tying and untying the leather thong keeping it closed. She was impatient to get things moving along and her frustration at the situation was bubbling over as she gazed out the carriage window in search of a bridge. Any bridge would do, but there wasn't a single one to be found. As the carriage drew to a stop, Edna once again gazed out the window at the wide expanse of water wondering why on earth the driver was leaving them in this spot. Frogs hopped about in the tall grasses along the water's edge in search of buzzing insects to fill their bellies. Ducks and geese glided through the water as other birds circled overhead occasionally diving into the Firth as they spied a fish from high above. All this beauty and not a single bridge in sight.

Angus stepped out of the carriage and extended a hand to help

Edna. "Thank ye," he said to the driver, who seemed eager to be on his way.

Edna turned to her husband. Sheer exasperation had her pinching her lips together. She spun around to view the ferries lined up along the banks and her hand went immediately to her forehead. "This cannae be. The only way across appears to be by way of a ferry."

"Is that no' a bridge of sorts?" Angus asked.

Edna's hand dropped from her head as her eyes went wide. "Did I no' tell ye ye're a genius?" Edna took his hand and hurried to the nearest ferryman. "Can ye take us across?"

He held out his hand for payment and Edna reached into her purse and removed another of her bottomless coin collection to hand him.

Once they were aboard and had traveled about halfway, Edna checked to be sure the ferryman wasn't paying attention to them. She motioned to Angus to put his arms around her. As he did, Edna closed her eyes and drew on her experiences at the bridge in Glendaloch to create a whirlwind of foggy mist that swirled around the two of them, taking care to make sure they stayed as far away from the ferryman as possible in order to not accidentally take him along on their journey. In her mind's eye, Edna pictured their destination and breathed deeply as she saw the boat heading through the mist and depositing them along the banks of another river. This time in France, or so she hoped.

"Where are we?" The man's shock was evident as his mouth gaped and his eyes seemed as though they might pop right out of his head.

"I doona ken," Edna said. It was an honest answer. They should be in France, but she couldn't be sure just yet. Wherever they had landed, the ferryman and his boat were still with them. Angus hopped off the ferry first and then placing his hands on her waist, lifted her onto the shore. "Ye'd best head back the same way. The fog must have taken ye off course."

"Aye. That must be it, but I've traveled this route every day for years. I've never seen this spot. Are ye sure ye wish to stay here?"

The man seemed very concerned about them, which Edna found endearing. She had faith that there were good people everywhere, if one only took the time to look.

"We'll be fine. Go on now. Head back to Edinburgh." Edna shushed him away with a wave of her hand.

The man pushed the boat away from the shore with his oar and as he did, he entered the swirling fog once again. Edna guided him with her mind until she knew he would be back where he belonged with an incredible story to tell anyone who'd listen.

Chuckling to herself, Edna turned to her husband who was wearing a large grin. "I doona ken about ye, but I'm getting tired. This has been a long day." Edna looked around the banks of the river and saw nothing but a dirt path leading away to who knew where. "Seems we've nae choice but to go this way. With luck we'll ken where we've landed before long."

Angus took her hand in his and they started on their way, but Edna stopped him. "I'm going to change into something a bit more comfortable." With a wave of her hands as she spun around twice, her clothing changed from her traveling outfit to one less cumbersome. Angus nodded his head in appreciation of the new look. Edna scanned him from head to toe, but decided that his Highland garb was acceptable for almost every instance, so she left him as he was and they headed off once again.

They'd been walking for what seemed hours and hadn't seen another soul to speak of. "I havenae walked this much in ages," Edna said, stopping beneath a shade tree to rest against its solid trunk. "How do we ken we're even heading in the right direction?"

"I suppose we doona." Angus leaned against the tree as he examined the sky. "The sun will be setting soon. I'd hoped we'd find a place to stay the night."

Edna was about to answer his concerns when the sound of horses and a carriage moving quickly could be heard just out of sight. A thick cloud of dust announced its approach as it topped the rise of the hill they'd just traversed.

Angus moved quickly into the middle of the dirt road.

"Will they stop?" Edna worried.

"Stay there," Angus ordered, as the carriage sped towards him. Waving his arms back and forth to signal the driver, he stood his ground.

Edna on the other hand was quite worried he would be run over and so she did what any good witch would do, she spelled the horses, forcing them to stop just short of Angus. She let out a sigh of relief and joined her husband as he approached the carriage.

The driver seemed quite perplexed as he hopped down from his perch muttering to himself in French. Edna wasn't fluent in the language and neither was Angus, so she cast another of her spells so they could understand and be understood by anyone they encountered.

The driver's complaints became clear to them as he cursed the four pure white horses who stood perfectly still as he examined them. He checked their hooves for stones and he checked their harnesses. When he could find nothing wrong, he scratched his head and turned to Angus.

"What have you done?" He was a smaller man and Angus towered over him, but that didn't seem to bother him in the least as he poked Angus with his finger.

"No' a thing," Angus answered, removing the man's finger. "Me wife and I are in need of a ride. Do ye think ye could help us with a ride to the nearest inn?"

"This is King Louis' carriage." He obviously felt this was an adequate answer to the request.

"Is he in there?" Edna asked, approaching the passenger compartment.

The man raced to stand in front of her before she could open the door. "No!"

"Sir, we would be most grateful if ye would help us," Edna said, all the while silently placing a spell on the driver. "We doona wish to be any trouble and nae one would have to ken."

The man's demeanor changed immediately. "Of course, Madame." He opened the door and waited for Edna and Angus to get inside. "There is an inn not far from here. I will take you."

"Thank ye... Ye havenae told us yer name." Edna said.

"Nicholas," he swept his arm across his midsection as he bowed.

"I am Lady Edna Campbell and this is me husband, Lord Angus Campbell. We have just arrived from Scotland.

"Welcome!" Nicholas said. He didn't seem to think it odd that he'd encountered them on the road in the middle of nowhere.

Edna couldn't help but believe that if he wasn't under her spell he would not have been quite so happy to help them. He closed the carriage door and climbed back up to his seat. Edna released the horses from her spell and they moved off smoothly. The driver kept them at a trot and not at the breakneck pace he'd been using when they stopped him. Edna relaxed back into the seat and took in the royal carriage. It was quite ornate, with gold and red accents. They were seated on soft velvet cushions hidden from the view of the outside world, with matching curtains that hung from the windows.

Edna took Angus' hand. "All will be well."

"Are ye saying that for me benefit or yers, me love?" Angus asked, a slight tinge of humor in his voice.

She couldn't help but laugh. Angus knew her so well. "For both of us," she assured him.

Peeking through the curtains of the carriage window, Edna noted that they'd stopped in front of a large three-story stone building. Tall, six-paned windows covered each floor. "Is this the inn?" she called to the driver.

He opened the carriage door. "The finest in all of Paris."

Edna took Angus' hand as she stepped out into the waning daylight, covering the city of Paris in a golden glow. "I'd like to see the Queen Mother," she said to the driver, who was still under her spell. She handed him a note quickly jotted down on their ride.

"Of course, Madame. I will request an audience for you and Lord Campbell."

"Good. Thank ye so much for delivering us safely."

He tipped his cap before climbing atop the carriage and heading off towards the palace.

# THREE

"That went well," Angus said as they entered their room.

"Ye sound surprised," Edna said. She ran her hand over the brocade bed covering on the large, wooden canopied bed.

"No' surprised. Impressed. It was quite a journey and ye managed to get us here in one piece."

Edna turned slowly, taking in the flowered wallpaper, carpeted floor and ornate wood furnishings. Finishing her visual exploration, she faced Angus with a victorious smile. "This is quite fun. I had me doubts when we found ourselves in the alley, but no' now."

"If this is an inn room, I can only imagine how elaborate the palace must be." Angus went to the window and peered out onto the courtyard they'd entered upon their arrival. "I'm hungry, Edna. Where will we find food?"

"I imagine there must be a dining room downstairs. Shall we go see?" She removed her cloak, laying it across the bed and then took the arm Angus offered. "Have I told ye how handsome ye look today?"

Angus puffed out his chest a bit more. A pleased smile appeared as he spoke. "Nae ye have no'."

"Well then, consider yerself told."

Angus placed a sweet kiss on Edna's lips. "Shall we?"

Despite its size, the dining room was cozy and warm. They were seated at a small round table near the fireplace. The table was set with fine silver utensils and pretty plates all set atop a lacy tablecloth. They seemed to be the only people eating.

"Where is everyone?" Edna asked the gentleman who came to their table.

"You are quite early Madame. The guests usually eat later."

"We've had a long journey and no' a thing to eat all day," Edna explained.

"Of course. I will bring you food and drink right away."

Dishes of game hens were placed in front of them along with bread, vegetables and a wonderful sauce. Wine was poured into goblets and set by their plates.

"Thank ye," Angus said.

The man bowed to them. "Enjoy your meal," he said as he walked away.

The food was better than Edna had expected. She noticed that Angus thought so, too. He'd cleaned his plate and was looking at hers.

"I'm no' going to finish it. Help yerself."

Angus switched plates with her and devoured every last drop, then leaned back in his chair seeming satisfied.

"We'll sleep well tonight I think," Edna said.

"Agreed," Angus said.

Edna sipped the last of her wine and wiped her lips with her napkin. "I hope the bed is comfortable."

"If no', I'm sure ye'll fix it." Angus winked.

"Tomorrow will be a busy day. Hopefully we'll meet everyone we need to meet and I'll have a better idea of what it is that I need to do to help Emilie."

"I have faith that ye will."

Edna appreciated Angus' confidence that she could do this, but despite her normal self-assuredness, she was having her doubts. A good night's sleep would probably fix that.

Angus stood and pulled her chair out for her. "Shall we?"

A smile appeared on Edna's lips. She'd be happy to snuggle up next to her man and enjoy their first night in Paris.

* * *

The following morning, much to Edna's surprise, the carriage was back. "Good morning," Nicholas said.

"Nicholas, we werenae expecting to see ye this morning." Edna and Angus had planned to walk to the palace. She wasn't sure they'd be allowed in, but thought it worth the attempt. It looked now as though they would have no problem whatsoever.

Nicholas bowed to them. "The Queen Mother would be pleased to see you this morning."

"That would be lovely," Edna said. Things were falling into place.

Nicholas opened the carriage door, ushering them in.

Edna elbowed Angus. "Me spell still seems to be working."

Angus placed his arm around her waist as he helped her up into the carriage. "I've been under yer spell since we first met."

"I had nae need to spell ye, Angus. Ye were quite willing if I recall." Edna settled into her seat and Angus joined her.

He chuckled. "Nae ye did no'."

The carriage moved through the city to the gates of Tuileries Palace. As they passed through, Edna could hardly contain her excitement. The immense structure was topped by a domed roof and matching cupola. Rows of windows extended out on either side of the magnificent entry they would soon be strolling through. Off in the distance, Edna could see the beautiful gardens of the palace and was absolutely beside herself at the thought of exploring them. She squeezed Angus' arm as the carriage pulled up at the palace entrance. Anticipation left her feeling abuzz with excitement.

"This way please." A liveried servant greeted them as they departed the carriage.

Following him in through the grand entry doors, Edna and Angus were amazed at the beauty of the palace. The massive expanse of the entryway seemed even larger when gazing up at the arched ceilings painted with colorful murals extending along the length of the wide corridor. Life-sized paintings of the royal family, past and present, lined the walls. Edna wanted to stop and admire each of them, but the liveryman continued swiftly in front of them and, not wanting to get lost, she followed him.

Everywhere they looked they were met with the beauty one would expect in the French court of this time. Edna glanced down at her dress, which she thought would be perfect for an audience with the Queen Mother, but that now seemed much too drab in comparison to those worn by the women they passed. Beautifully embroidered fabrics in varying pastel shades were everywhere and the women wearing them moved with a regal grace befitting those who walked the halls of the palace. The men were also dressed in resplendent attire that included silky stockings worn over breaches fitted just below the knee and embroidered waistcoats with matching cravats. Coats with full skirts to the knee were the finishing touch on most of their outfits.

As they reached the open doors to the salon, Edna peeked in and noticed quite a few people milling about. "The Queen Mother will be here soon," the servant said as he left them to enter on their own.

"I wonder which one of these people is Emilie." Edna said.

"It may be easier to find Robert MacMillan," Angus noted as he motioned with his head towards a group of men dressed in kilts on the other side of the vast room.

Two thrones, covered in tufted red velvet, were positioned on a dais centered along the wall and facing the door. Drapes of gold and red brocaded fabric hung from a large ornate gold crown centered above. The rest of the room was more subdued than the hall they'd just traversed and yet was still beautifully decorated with paintings and statues. It gave all the focus in the salon to the thrones where the Queen Mother and her son would sit when they arrived.

Edna and Angus walked around the room nodding to those in attendance that morning. No one seemed particularly interested in speaking with them. They were all there for one purpose and that was to see the Queen Mother, Marie de Medici.

They made their way over to the kilted group.

"Good morn to ye," Angus said. "I be Angus Campbell and this is me wife, Edna."

"Good morn," the men replied.

"We're looking for Robert MacMillan. Would ye ken where we might find him?"

The tallest of the men spoke. "He's with the young king."

"I see. Where might that be?" Angus asked.

"It's hard to say." He glanced around to the other men in the group, who shrugged their shoulders.

"Then they would no' be joining the Queen Mother this morning?"

"'Tis no' likely. My guess is they are outdoors, possibly riding along the banks of the river."

"Thank ye. We'll see him later then."

If the men were curious about Angus and Edna, they didn't show it as they went back to their conversation.

Edna was about to say something when the room came alive with excited voices. The Queen Mother entered the room with her entourage and made her way to the throne. Those present created an aisle for her, bowing and curtsying as she passed. Marie was dressed in an elaborate gown in a shade of deep burgundy. Creamy, ivory-colored pearls encircled her throat and, also dropped from her ears. A pleated white lace collar attached to her gown and stood firmly behind her head, framing her hair which was worn up and studded with jewels.

Marie begrudgingly acknowledged a few of those waiting as she passed. Once she was seated, a semi-circle was formed by those who'd been waiting and one-by-one they presented themselves to her. Some she knew well and she spoke to them in lowered tones, keeping their conversations private. Others were new to her, as evidenced by their nervous fidgeting as they stood before her.

When it was time for Edna and Angus to approach, they made their way up the steps of the dais. Edna curtsied and Angus bowed.

"Good morning, Yer Highness. I am Lady Edna Campbell and this is me husband, Lord Angus Campbell."

"You speak for your husband," Marie noted.

Edna hadn't thought about the protocols of the time and whether or not it was acceptable for her to be the one speaking to the Queen Mother. "Me apologies, I..."

Marie held up a hand to Edna. "Do not worry, my dear. It pleases me when a woman shows her worth."

Edna breathed a silent sigh of relief, tipping her head to the Queen Mother and smiling.

"You are here from Scotland." It was a statement, not a question.

"Aye. We are."

"Why did you wish to see me?" Marie tipped her head slightly, her curiosity showing.

Edna hadn't given that much thought either and was going to be flying by the seat of her pants here. "When in Paris, it is incumbent upon us to pay our respects and those of King James, to let ye ken that Scotland looks fondly on all of France, but especially the royal family."

Marie seemed pleased with this answer. "Where are you staying?"

"At a lovely inn no' far from here. Le Rosier."

The Queen Mother sniffed at this. "Ah, yes, Monsieur Rose." Marie said the man's name with disdain and a wrinkling of her nose, which quickly came and went. "You are welcome to explore the gardens and to join us later this evening. We will be announcing the betrothal of one of my ladies."

"We would be pleased to offer our congratulations. Is she here now?" Edna held herself in check. She had to stop herself from asking if the young lady was Emilie Toussaint. Tipping her hand at this point would cause more problems than necessary.

"She is in the gardens with her betrothed, the Comte Matteo Barbieri." Marie looked pleased with herself as she said. "I arranged the marriage agreement."

Edna couldn't help but look towards the windows for a moment to search for Emilie. Luckily, Marie interpreted her distraction as interest in the grounds.

A brief lull in the conversation was followed by Marie dismissing them. "Off with you then. Walk the gardens. They are quite beautiful."

Looking past them, Marie nodded to someone behind them who obviously was waiting for an audience. Edna and Angus took their leave and headed for the open doors they assumed would lead to the gardens.

"It seems we'll have our work cut out for us. The Queen Mother made this match and she is the only one who can change its course. Let's go find Emilie, shall we?"

"Lead the way, me love," Angus stood by the door allowing Edna to pass through before him. Once down the steps and onto the *grande allée du jardin des Tuileries* that would lead them through the garden, Edna and Angus stopped for a moment to get their bearings. Marie had been right, the gardens were a spectacular sight. Greenery lined the path on both sides, accompanied by the fragrant smell of roses. The garden was divided into several rectangles filled with colorful flowers and shrubs and separated by pathways for walking.

As they strolled arm-in-arm, Edna spied a young woman walking along with an older man. "That must be Emilie," Edna said, picking up her pace as she headed straight towards them.

"How can ye tell?" Angus asked, keeping up with her.

"I cannae. I'm just guessing."

Angus chuckled on hearing this.

Edna gave him the look. The one she saved for when she wasn't having any of his shenanigans. "Well, there's nae way to be sure from this distance. We must meet them."

As they approached, the couple turned towards them. Edna put the brakes on and slowed to a crawl, smiling brightly at them. "Good day to ye," she said.

"Good day," the gentlemen bobbed his head in greeting.

"'Tis a beautiful garden. We just met with the Queen Mother and she told us we simply must explore it."

"It is the perfect day to do so," the man said.

"I'm Lord Angus Campbell and this is me wife, Edna." Edna was grateful that Angus made the introductions. She'd been so focused on getting to Emilie she'd completely forgotten all of the niceties involved with meeting people you didn't know.

"I am Comte Matteo Barbieri and this is my betrothed, Emilie Toussaint."

Edna had to keep herself from jumping for joy. They'd found her. Now all they had to do was convince all parties that it would be in their best interest to allow Emilie to marry for love and not as part of an arrangement that would benefit the Queen Mother, the Comte and, she imagined, Emilie's family. "Emilie, I was hoping to meet ye."

"Is this true?" Emilie asked. A young woman in her early twenties, with pretty honey-colored curls and a sweet face, she seemed a bit shy and reserved.

"Why aye, it is. We wanted to congratulate ye on yer betrothal. The Queen Mother told us all about it."

Seeming less than enthusiastic, Emilie replied. "Thank you."

"Will you attend the reception the Queen Mother has arranged for this evening?" Barbieri asked.

"We will be there," Edna said. She eyed Emilie. "Did ye happen to see the glorious full moon the other night?"

Emilie's mood shifted from solemn to curious. "I did, Madame Campbell."

"Wasnae it beautiful? Do ye ken, I've heard if ye make a wish on the night of the full moon that it will be granted."

Emilie's eyes widened as a hopeful smile lit her lips. "I had not heard," Emilie said.

"Aye, 'tis true, or so they say."

Angus took Edna's cue and engaged the Comte in conversation. The two men wandered further into the garden, leaving Edna alone with Emilie.

"I am here to help ye, me dear," Edna said, once the men were out of earshot.

Emilie's hands flew to her mouth as her eyes filled with happy tears. "Bless you, Madame Campbell."

"Call me Edna, please. It may take some time to sort this all out, but in the end ye will marry the man ye wish and no' the Comte."

"My only wish is to marry Robert MacMillan." Her shoulders slumped and her demeanor returned to sadness once again. "I have spoken to the Queen Mother, but she will not allow it and my father agrees. Robert is a soldier and I am the daughter of a Comte. It is not possible for me to marry him."

"Nonsense. Ye can and ye will." Edna's determination and confidence were on full display.

"You are so sure of yourself, Madame."

"'Tis me job and one I'm verra good at, if I doona say so meself. I've matched many couples. Ye are here. Robert is here. This will be a piece of cake. Leave it in me hands and yer wish will come true. In the meantime, go along with the plans that have been made for ye."

"The Comte is a good man. He has been very kind to me, but I can tell he doesn't love me any more than I love him."

"That will make me job much easier." Edna lifted Emilie's chin with her hand. "Do ye trust me?"

"I do." Emilie looked up to the sky. Through the morning light it was still possible to see a faint portion of the moon. "The moon has worked some magic that I do not understand."

"No' many do. Let's just say it was a combination of things. I believe ye received a stone from Madame DuBois."

"Yes. Do you know her?" Emilie asked.

"We've never met, but ye see it was Madame DuBois, the stone, and the full moon that caused yer heartfelt plea to travel across time, all the way to Edinburgh in the year 2022 to reach me, and lucky for ye it did. I cannae say nae to love."

"You are from the future?"

"Aye. I've traveled far just for ye," Edna said as she gazed into Emilie's eyes with what she hoped Emilie would see as a sign that she really was there to help.

"I am amazed and happy that it is so."

Edna noted the relieved tears that sprung to Emilie's eyes. She took out her hankie and handed it to the lass. A sense of purpose and satisfaction overcame her as she too became somewhat emotional. "All will be well, me dear. Let me do me work and before ye ken it ye will have yer man."

Emilie bowed her head briefly in apparent acknowledge-ment. "I am blessed. Thank you."

They continued walking as Emilie dabbed at her cheeks with the hankie before holding her head high as she got a hold of herself. They caught up with Angus and Matteo who had stopped near a pool of water and were engaged in conversation.

"Angus, we should be on our way," Edna said as they approached.

"We will see you this evening." Matteo said.

"Aye. We wouldnae miss the opportunity to wish ye well." Angus shook Matteo's hand and bowed slightly in Emilie's direction. "Shall we?" He held out his arm for Edna to take.

Edna peeked back over her shoulder at Emilie who was once again walking along with the Comte. "This went well. Our mission should be complete in nae time."

"It seems the Comte is no' keen to marry," Angus said.

"What do ye mean?" Edna asked.

"We spoke for some time. Each time I mentioned Emilie his mood changed. When I asked him if he was happy to marry her, he surprised me. It seems that the Comte is a bit of a miser. When I pressed him, he confessed that he did no' wish to marry. He is only doing so because the Queen Mother arranged it. The last thing he wants is a wife. It is an expense he does no' wish to incur."

"Oh, my. We must make sure they do no' marry then. Nae matter what happens with Robert and Emilie, she must no' marry this man."

"He is no' unkind. He enjoys Emilie's company and he would be good to her, but as he told me, he is frugal and a wife is an expense he does no' wish to have."

"He's so much older than Emilie. He must be her father's age or older."

"And he has avoided marriage to this point. Perhaps ye can make his wish come true as well."

"I believe we can fix it all. Emilie will have her heart's desire and Comte Matteo Barbieri will have his money."

CHAPTER

# FOUR

As they walked away from the palace, Edna stopped. "I must see Madame DuBois."

Angus lifted an eyebrow in puzzlement. "Who?"

"The woman who helped Emilie with her wish. I thought ye'd ken that."

"I dinna ken her name." Angus explained. "Why do ye need to see her?"

Edna lowered her voice to just above a whisper. She glanced around before speaking, making sure no one could hear her. "I wanted to let her ken we are here and to thank her for helping Emilie. It's good for her to ken she's no' alone. And, ye never ken, I may need her help. It's always good to check in with the local witch or witches as the case may be. We are, after all, in a time when witches are no' appreciated for the good they can do."

He crossed his arms over his chest. "Is it really a good idea to see her? If something goes wrong it could go wrong for both of ye."

Edna loved that he was so concerned for her, but she felt it was necessary and so they would find her. "She'll be able to tell me where I need to be careful and what to watch out for."

"I hadnae thought about that. Ye could be putting yourself in more danger than I originally thought."

"That's why I've got ye with me." Edna leaned into Angus giving him a playful bump.

"I doona like it but if ye insist, I ken I cannae change yer mind. Ye'd do well to no' be out of me sight."

"I promise to steer clear of precarious situations, me love."

Angus harrumphed.

"What? Do ye no' believe me?"

"'Tis no' whether or no' I believe ye. Danger seems to find ye nae matter which direction ye steer yerself."

Edna chuckled. "Oh, Angus darlin'. I do love ye so." She touched her head to his arm as they walked. He was her rock, her steadiness and, if she were being honest with herself, she couldn't do this without him. "I think it's this way." Edna had honed in on Madame DuBois and set a path through the streets of Paris by following her instincts.

"How do ye ken where she is?" Angus wondered.

Edna tapped her temple with one finger. "I just ken."

Angus picked up his pace as Edna moved decisively down a street here and an alley there before stopping in front of a small home that was in great need of repair.

"This is it," Edna said, approaching the door. She knocked lightly and hearing shuffling coming from inside, knocked again.

"Yes," a voice called from inside.

"Madame DuBois?" Edna answered.

The door opened and Madame DuBois gazed first at Edna and then Angus. "Who are you?" Her voice was tinged with suspicion.

"I'm Edna Campbell and this is me husband Angus. We are here from the future. From the Council of Witches in Edinburgh."

Madame DuBois stepped back, narrowing her eyes as she examined them further. "What do you want with me?"

"Doona worry. We're only here to introduce ourselves and to let ye ken that we are working on Emilie Toussaint's behalf. And, by the way, thank ye for helping her." She smiled warmly at the woman, waiting for an indication that she felt they could be trusted.

"Come in." Madame DuBois swept her arm out, indicating that they were welcome inside.

Edna moved through the door, followed by Angus who had to duck his head to avoid hitting it on the door frame.

"Please sit," Madame DuBois motioned to two wooden chairs set beside a table.

"I'll stand," Angus said, eyeing the tiny chairs.

"I told the young lady not to tell anyone about me." Madame DuBois scowled and shook her head.

"Doona be angry with her. She did no' give ye away and we willnae endanger ye."

Madame DuBois seemed a bit skeptical as she rolled her eyes heavenward.

"I promise," Edna said. "I understand yer vulnerability during these times. I will protect ye."

The woman relaxed, releasing a breath. "I need one of these," she teased, indicating Angus. "What is it you want?"

"I just wanted to introduce meself, let ye ken yer magic worked and ask for yer help if I need it while I'm here." Edna did her best to keep her voice light and friendly. Madame DuBois obviously needed reassurance that they meant no harm.

"You're a witch. Why would you need my help?" Madame DuBois said.

"'Tis true. I am. I doona have anything in mind at the moment, but I couldnae bring a lot of me things with me." Edna looked around the room at the neat row of bottles, some with liquid, some with herbs and some with powdery substances. "If I need to concoct a potion or need herbs for a spell it would be good to ken that I can come to ye."

Madame DuBois wasn't being resistant, but she wasn't exactly being receptive either.

"I'll only ask ye if it's absolutely necessary," Edna assured her.

She blew out a resigned breath. "All right. I will help if I can."

"Thank ye." Edna was relieved she'd broken through the barrier Madame DuBois had erected to protect herself.

Her tone became more friendly as she sat down across from Edna. "You say you are from the future." A genuine curiosity could be heard in the sound of her voice.

"Aye, the twenty-first century. Can ye believe it?" It was even surprising to Edna who had time traveled often enough to know it could be done, but was still amazed that it was possible.

"I am having some difficulty with it, but the Council of Witches is powerful, are they not?" Madame DuBois straightened her spine and gave her full attention to Edna.

"Ye could say that. We have members in every place and time."

"There is a council house nearby. I have never been."

"Do ye ken where it is?" Edna asked, surprised to hear this.

"It is in the countryside outside of the city. I have never felt the need to visit, but if necessary I will find it."

Edna was relieved to hear this. She'd been worried about Madame DuBois. Witches were not treated kindly and were often killed in this time period. At times without any evidence against them at all. "Do ye ken if the council house ye speak of is the headquarters in this time?"

"I'm afraid I don't know. I am a witch who knows little about those things." Madame DuBois seemed more relaxed in their company now that she'd had some time to get to know them. "I will make us tea."

"We would love that, but we must return to our inn. We are attending a reception tonight at the palace."

"Oh, what is happening there?" Madame DuBois asked.

"A celebration of the betrothal of Emilie Toussaint and Matteo Barbieri."

Madame DuBois scowled on hearing this. "You will fix this, no?"

"I will fix this, aye. And now we must be on our way."

"Goodbye and good luck." She kissed Edna on both cheeks.

Angus had to bend down so she could reach him. She gave his arms an extra squeeze. "Strong," she said with appreciation.

Edna giggled under her breath. She was very aware that other women found her husband handsome, but he was hers and always would be.

❧

THE RECEPTION at the palace that evening was attended by many important figures from what Edna could see. Emilie stood beside Comte Barbieri, the Queen Mother and her favorite, Concino Concini. They greeted their guests, who waited in line to offer their congratulations to the betrothed.

Edna noted that Emilie seemed very far away as she nodded and thanked those who spoke with her. Her focus was on something or someone on the other side of the room. Following her gaze, Edna saw what her distraction was. The man who was the focus of Emilie's gaze was over six feet tall, wore his long, dark hair loose, had a strong jawline and aquiline nose. He was quite handsome in Edna's estimation. "Angus, I believe that must be our Robert. Ye should go speak with him."

Angus took a moment to locate the man she was speaking of and then left her side, making his way across the crowded room to Robert MacMillan. Edna noted that Emilie and Robert stared longingly at each other and then abruptly looked away as another well-wisher greeted her and the Comte.

When it was Edna's turn, she greeted Barbieri and Emilie with her congratulations.

"We're so happy you could come," Barbieri said. "Where is your husband? I enjoyed meeting him today and was looking forward to seeing you both tonight."

"He saw a tartan across the room and couldnae resist visiting with a fellow Highlander. I'm sure he'll be along soon." Edna pointed to Angus on the other side of the room.

"No matter, I will speak with him when he is free." Matteo glanced at his betrothed. "The greetings have gone on too long. Shall we?" He offered his arm to Emilie who walked away with him.

"They make a lovely couple, don't they," the Queen Mother said as she joined Edna.

"She is so young and he is such a mature man," Edna replied. She purposely didn't say he was an old man even though in her mind he was forty years older than Emilie.

Marie tipped her head seeming surprised that Edna might disagree with her.

Edna, not wishing to alienate Marie, quickly added, "But aye, they do. They are both verra handsome."

Marie smiled. "I am pleased you think so. I am never mistaken when it comes to matters of love."

*Neither am I.* Edna kept that thought to herself.

"Tell me, Madame Campbell. Are you enjoying your stay in Paris?"

"I am. Verra much. Angus and I have long wanted to visit and when the opportunity arose, we were ecstatic." Understanding that the way to Marie's heart was with compliments, Edna continued. "Yer palace is the most beautiful I have seen and yer gardens are exquisite. Angus and I were just saying how much we've been enjoying our stay."

"Have I introduced you to Concino?" Marie asked, beckoning him to join them. "He is a good friend of Matteo's."

Concino gave a slight bow in Edna's direction.

"Concino Concini, this is Madame Edna Campbell from Scotland."

"It is lovely to meet you," he said. "Where in Scotland are you from?"

"Edinburgh," Edna said, smiling warmly. "Have ye been?"

"No. Although I hope to visit someday." He glanced at Marie.

"Why would you wish to? Madame Campbell has just told me that this is the most beautiful palace she has ever seen."

Concini raised an eyebrow at Marie. "If you'll excuse me." He left them and wandered off towards a group of gentlemen who had gathered together and seemed to be having a very animated conversation. Unfortunately they were just far enough away that it was not possible to hear what they were discussing.

Marie walked off in the other direction with a shake of her head and without another word, leaving Edna alone and wondering what that was all about.

~

"She's quite beautiful, do ye no' think?" Angus said, referring to Emilie.

"Aye." Robert MacMillan seemed quite the lovestruck lad. Although he was surrounded by other Highlanders, it was as if he were on an island alone and adrift in a sea of people. It seemed his sole focus was on the young lady who stood only across the room, and yet seemed a million miles away.

Angus observed Robert carefully as he appeared to reluctantly look away from Emilie and Matteo.

"If I were a young, unmarried man like yerself, I might be tempted to pursue her." Getting to know Robert and his feelings for Emilie was his task. Robert wasn't giving him much more than wistful glances her way. Despite this, Angus thought there was love in those looks.

"That would no' be possible," Robert said, putting an end to the conversation. "She's a Comte's daughter. I am a soldier."

Angus wouldn't push him into more conversation about Emilie. That would come, but this wasn't the time or place. "Robert, I understand that ye are one of the young king's guards."

"I am." He reluctantly turned to Angus.

It was hard to tell whether Robert wished to continue speaking with him. His attention darted back and forth between Emilie and

Angus, but Angus knew he needed to get Robert to confide in him and so he pressed on. "What does that entail?"

"He's a young lad, so much of me time is spent making sure he doesnae get himself into trouble."

"Do ye enjoy it?" Angus asked.

Robert nodded. "He can be a challenge, but I enjoy me time with him. I am no' his mother, so I cannae stop him from doing as he wishes, but he listens to reason."

"Having once been a young lad meself, ye have me sympathy." Angus chuckled and was happy when Robert joined him.

"He enjoys riding. We visit the stables almost daily, ye should join us," Robert suggested.

"I would like that." Angus wanted to be helpful to Edna and befriending Robert was a good start.

Robert seemed happy to hear it. "I have nae doubt that Louis would enjoy meeting ye. He's a curious lad. He'll have many questions for ye I'm sure."

"I look forward to answering them. Unfortunately, I do no' have a horse with me."

"That is no' an issue," Robert said. "There are many to choose from in the stable. I'll have one saddled and ready for ye when ye arrive."

"Thank ye. That's most kind of ye."

Robert's gaze slid toward Emilie who was now being led around the room by Matteo.

"Ye cannae take yer eyes from her," Angus noted.

"As ye have said, she is beautiful. I do no' seem to be able to help meself," Robert admitted.

"If a miracle occurred and ye could be with her, would ye?" Angus already knew the answer to this question, but he wanted to hear what Robert would say.

"It would take a miracle, sir, but aye." Robert seemed reluctant to look away from Emilie, but he faced Angus giving him his full attention.

"Ye have spent time with her, have ye no'?" Angus asked.

Robert stiffened and eyed Angus with suspicion. "Why would ye ask that?"

"I want to help, if possible."

"To answer yer question, aye. Now that she is betrothed that will end." His voice softened and became barely audible. "I will see to it."

Angus felt the lad's pain. If he couldn't be with Edna he wasn't sure what he would do. "I'm sorry to hear it. I am always on the side of love."

"Are ye married?" Robert asked.

"Me wife is right over there." Angus pointed to Edna with pride. "I love her with all me heart and soul."

"Then ye're a lucky man," Robert said, following Angus' outstretched finger.

"I agree wholeheartedly and I wish the same for ye, lad."

"Thank ye, but I doona ken that I believe love is in me future. I've been given a glimpse of what love is and now unfortunately it is being taken from me."

Angus felt the need to give the lad some hope. Edna could give him more than hope, but it wouldn't happen immediately. "The lass does no' wish for this marriage. Ye must ken that."

"She may no' wish it, but her father and the Queen Mother are determined that she will marry this old man." There was a tinge of anger and resentment in Robert's voice.

"I doona believe *the old man,* as ye call him, wishes the marriage either." Angus tried not to take offense to Robert's words. He understood the lad's frustration, but as an older gentleman himself, those words stung. He, of course, wasn't nearly as old as Matteo and yet he felt protective kinship with his new friend.

Robert's eyes lit up on hearing this. "How do ye ken it?"

"He told me when we spoke earlier." Angus gazed at Matteo who stood with Emilie. He was attentive to her, but in a grandfatherly way. "I feel they are both being forced into a marriage that neither wants."

Resigned as he was to the outcome, Robert was doing an excellent job of hiding his true feelings. "Still there is no' a thing that can be done to stop it."

Angus knew there was always something that could be done and that Edna would do whatever it took to make it happen, but he would keep that information to himself for the moment.

As Matteo and Emilie continued greeting guests at the reception, they were getting closer and closer to Robert and Angus.

"I must leave," Robert said. "Meet me at the stable tomorrow morning. I look forward to riding with ye." He hurried off before Angus could answer him.

Angus turned to look for Edna and was immediately met by Matteo and Emilie.

"There you are," Matteo said. A warm smile greeted Angus as though they were old friends. "Who was that you were speaking with?"

"Robert MacMillan. He is a guard to King Louis," Angus explained.

"You spoke with him for quite a long time," Matteo said.

Angus was amused and confused that Matteo had been watching him and calculating the length of time he spoke with Robert. "When with a fellow Scot, there are always stories to tell. Do ye ken him?"

"No. We've not met. Emilie, do you know him?" Matteo asked.

Emilie seemed startled out of her malaise on hearing this question. "No. Why would I know him?"

"He is here at the palace, as are you." Matteo's gaze fell on Emilie and lingered there.

Angus thought he heard a hint of suspicion in the older man's question.

Emilie felt it too. "I spend most of my time with the Queen Mother. I rarely have time to meet with others at the palace."

"Have ye seen Edna?" Angus decided it would be a good idea to change the focus of their conversation.

"She was just over there a moment ago," Emilie said, peering over her shoulder.

"I see her. Will ye excuse me?" Angus asked.

"Of course," Matteo said.

"Enjoy the rest of yer celebration." Angus nodded to them both and headed straight for Edna.

"How did yer chat with Robert go?" Edna asked when he reached her.

"Good. 'Tis obvious he is a man in love. I believe they've been meeting secretly up until this point. He claims he will no' see her again now that she is betrothed."

"Hmmm... Do ye believe him?" Edna asked.

"I cannae say that I do, although it would be best if they dinna see each other until this was all sorted out. I think Matteo may be suspicious of them."

"Really? Why would ye think that?" Edna asked.

"Nae reason in particular. It's just a feeling that I have."

"Matteo seems to have taken a liking to ye. It could come in handy for our purposes."

"He seems out of place here in the palace. I ken he is a friend to the Medici family and Concini, but I doona believe there is a real friendship there. I will say, though, I like the man. He is honest and straightforward in his conversation. I feel for him."

"That's one of the things I love about ye, Angus. Ye've a kind heart."

"The man needs a friend and while we are in this time, I will do me best to be his friend." He wrinkled his brow before speaking again. "I cannae help but wonder why he has agreed to this marriage though. It is clear he would rather remain unencumbered by a wife."

"Unencumbered?" Edna gave him a sideways look that said she disapproved of the word.

"I'm speaking of Matteo, me love. I have never felt encumbered by ye, me lovely wife."

"Ye'd best no' be," Edna teased.

Angus rolled his eyes at her silliness. "I'm ready to retire. Are ye?"

"Most certainly."

"I'm going to ride with Robert and Louis tomorrow morning. I'll need a good night's sleep."

"Thank ye for helping me, love." Edna wrapped her arm around his, getting as close as possible.

"Doona tempt me, lass. I did tell ye I need a good night's sleep," Angus said, knowing exactly what Edna was up to.

CHAPTER

# FIVE

A seventeen-hand shining black steed awaited Angus when he joined Robert at the stables.

"What a beauty," Angus said. He examined the horse, running his hands along its flanks. "Are ye sure this one's for me?"

"He is."

"It's been a while since I've ridden a horse as fine as this," Angus said. The horse had a mane and tail that shined like glass in the sunlight and fell almost to the ground. Perfectly groomed and trained, it would be a privilege to ride a horse this fine.

Robert mounted his horse, a large grey of the same stature. Angus joined Robert as he took stock of the fine leather saddle and reins he would be using.

"His Majesty will join us shortly," Robert said.

They rode around the arena located next to the stables. Angus found a sense of relaxation and peace as he rode. The horse was very responsive to his commands, easily moving into an extended trot alongside Robert and his horse. It had been ages since he'd ridden for the pure joy of it. He followed Robert's lead as they rode in sync with each other.

"Beautiful!" King Louis XIII had arrived without fanfare. His horse, a brilliant white, had the same regal stature as the ones ridden by Robert and Angus. "Let me warm him up and I will join you," he said.

"Of course, sire," Robert said.

"Robert, I have told you before. Call me by my name please."

"Louis," Robert said as his mouth curled into a half smile.

"Who is this?" Louis asked, pointing to Angus.

"Angus Campbell, at yer service," Angus said. Louis was exactly as Angus had pictured him. A young teen dressed in the finest garments of pale blue silk and satin embroidered with gold thread. His doublet was decorated with ornamental ribbons coiled into flowers at the waist. Tabbed panels that extended below his midsection were bound with wide satin binding. He wore a matching cloak that hung loosely over one shoulder, cradling his arm. It was tied across his chest, holding it in place. The lining was a matching patterned fabric that was meant to catch the eye. His breeches were tied below the knee with more ribbon to hold them fast. Louis' boots were cuffed at the top and he wore spurs fastened above the heel. His hair was long and curled in the fashion of the day.

"You are visiting from Scotland. Are you Robert's uncle?" Louis asked, seeming genuinely interested.

"Nae. We only met yesterday. We are countrymen and so we have a bond in that way," Angus explained.

Louis nodded as he took his horse to a trot and then a gallop. When he slowed beside Angus, he said. "I'm pleased to meet you. Shall we all three make our horses dance?"

"I'm afraid I'm nae as accomplished as Yer Highness in the equestrian arts."

Louis accepted this with a knowing smile. "We shall teach you then. Watch and then join us."

Robert and Louis rode their horses side-by-side in a *pas de deux*. The beautiful fluidity of the movements was breathtaking. The more he watched, the more Angus wanted to give it a try himself.

The horses stopped alongside him. "Are ye ready?" Robert asked.

"Aye. I'm eager to try." Angus was an experienced horseman, but he rode to travel from one place to the next or, when he'd been a young man, for battle. This was something completely new to him and he wondered if he was ready for the challenge it presented.

He needn't have worried. His horse was well-schooled and followed along with little input from Angus.

"We need music," Louis said, glancing around. "Where are my musicians?"

"They arenae here this morning," Robert said.

Louis' face transformed from a disappointed pout to a mischievous grin. "Perhaps you can sing, Robert."

Robert chuckled at this. "I doona wish to scare the horses."

It was obvious to Angus that Louis and Robert had a good relationship. They bantered back and forth, teasing and laughing. Angus wasn't immune to their teasing. He found himself more than once being targeted by Louis. He took no offense. It was all done in good humor and he appreciated that he was being accepted by none other than the king himself. After they'd practiced their *pas de deux* plus one several times, they left the arena and rode the aisles of the garden at a stately walk.

Louis turned to Angus. "What do you think of a man who loves a woman but will not tell her?"

"It depends on the circumstances," Angus said, slightly taken aback by the question.

Louis adjusted himself in the saddle and checked his posture to a more perfect line. "The circumstances are that he does not believe he is good enough for her."

"Louis..." Robert tried to interrupt.

"And so he watches her from afar," Louis finished.

"Well, I think he should take a chance and tell her how he feels. He might be surprised to find she feels the same way," Angus replied. He was enjoying Louis. The young man obviously had opinions about everything. He was the king after all. It showed his great affection for Robert that he cared so much about his love life.

"That is what I have told him." Louis looked to Robert.

"Are we speaking of Robert?" Angus asked, knowing full well they were.

"We are."

"Louis, ye ken she is to marry Barbieri," Robert said, his exasperation evident.

"He is old enough to be her grandfather," Louis protested.

"Nonetheless, yer mother is the one who has arranged the marriage." It seemed Robert thought that would put an end to the topic.

"I can speak with her. She will listen to me," Louis continued.

"And what of her father, the Comte?" Robert asked. "Will ye speak to him as well?"

"He will do whatever my mother tells him to do." Louis appeared quite pleased with himself.

Robert's voice became somber. "Emilie deserves more than I have to offer her."

"Angus, what do you think?" Louis asked.

"I think love has a strange way of finding those who need it most."

"Robert needs it," Louis said.

"Then he shall have it," Angus assured him.

"Good."

Magic alone wouldn't solve Emilie and Robert's problem and so Angus was pleased the young king would be an advocate for them with his mother. Whether she would listen to him or not was another question all together. Still, it was hopeful news he would share with Edna.

They rode back to the stable where they were greeted by an entourage of people waiting for Louis. He dismounted, leaving his horse for Robert to unsaddle and put away, then walked away followed by those waiting to fuss over him as they made their way back to the palace.

"He's quite something," Angus noted. "I like him."

Robert took each saddle, cleaning his and Louis'. Angus cleaned his own and then they toweled down the horses before putting them away in their stalls and leaving them each with a bucket of oats.

"Thank ye for allowing me to join ye," Angus said.

"It was a pleasure to have ye with us. I ken Louis enjoyed yer company, as did I."

"I'm happy to hear it."

"Shall we get something to eat?" Robert asked.

"I'd like that." Angus followed him towards the palace kitchen where they would enjoy a fine meal and good wine.

WHILE ANGUS WAS busy with Robert, Edna called on Emilie. They walked through the streets of Paris enjoying the fine sunny day they had been gifted with. Vendors along their path sold everything from food and drink, to fine items of clothing, bolts of fabric, and household goods.

They stopped at a small shop selling books. Edna loved seeing the volumes of brand-new books alongside some older well-loved books with worn bindings and tattered pages. She thought she might come back and purchase something to take back home with her, but that could wait. She had more important things to tend to.

"Emilie, tell me about Robert," Edna said. She wanted to be sure that theirs was a love that Edna should see to fruition.

The young lady blushed, placing her hand on her cheek as if to cool it down.

Edna took her arm and walked back out of the shop and onto the street.

"He is the most wonderful man I've ever met. He is handsome, kind, generous and..." She didn't go on.

Edna understood. He meant everything to Emilie. "Have ye had a chance to speak with him?"

"Many times in the past. We've walked together in the garden. He's brought me beautiful flowers and he has spoken to me in ways that make my heart beat faster and my head spin."

"What happened to end this?" Edna asked. She thought she knew, but wanted to hear it from Emilie.

The joyful blush drained from her cheeks, "My father decided it was time for me to marry. He spoke with Her Highness and a marriage was arranged with Matteo."

"I ken that ye doona wish to marry him." Edna glanced at the now saddened Emilie. "I'm sorry. I dinna wish to upset ye. I can see how difficult this is for ye."

"It is not my decision, though I wish that it was." Her eyelashes fluttered as she looked away from Edna.

What Edna was about to say was not going to be what she wanted to say or what Emilie wanted to hear. "I must ask ye to continue to agree to this marriage."

Emilie put her hand on her belly, obviously distressed by what she'd just heard.

Edna grasped her hand and gazed into her eyes. "Ye need no' be happy about it, but I promise ye that I am here to help. Ye will no' marry Barbieri, of that I am sure." She wasn't really, but Edna's record of matching happy couples was a good one. Some might even say it was excellent, but this situation was different. She hadn't matched this couple. They'd matched themselves and circumstances were making it impossible for them to be together. Edna would do her best to fix this situation for them. Only time would tell if it would work out the way she hoped it would. In the meantime, it would be important for Emilie to continue the ruse. "Do ye think ye can do that?"

"If it means a lifetime with Robert, I can do anything." Her lips curved slightly in a shy smile.

"Good." Edna's nose was drawn to a small bakery. "Mmmm... I love the smell of freshly baked bread."

"Shall we get some?" Emilie asked. Apparently the idea of eating a fine loaf of bread brought her joy because she was now beaming with happiness.

Edna entered the small shop and glanced around at the different loaves. "Which is best?" she asked, glancing at Emilie.

"*Pain mollet*." She pointed to the small round loaves stacked against each other.

"We'll have two, please," Edna said.

The man tending the shop handed them two small loaves and Edna obliged with coins from her purse. Once outside, she tore a piece of the bread and placed it in her mouth, amazed what good flavor it had. It was salty, but not too salty. The interior was soft and spongy and altogether very flavorful. As an added bonus, it was still warm from the oven.

"Do you like it?" Emilie asked.

Edna covered her mouth before speaking. "Verra much."

"Do you eat bread in your time?" Emilie put a dainty bite of bread into her mouth.

"I do. There are so many different varieties, but I've no' tried something like this."

They walked on, each enjoying their small loaf of bread. When they came to the river and walked along its banks, Edna noticed that Emilie drew closer and in almost a whisper said, "Tell me about the future."

"What would ye like to ken? There's a lot to tell." Edna was happy that their earlier conversation was now in the past and Emilie seemed more animated in her words and actions.

"Everything. I wish to know everything."

"It is filled with wonderful things that ye would be amazed by. There is a box you can hold in your hand that contains thousands, no millions of books. Speaking to people who are far away is possible with something called a telephone. So many things. It would take me hours to explain all them to ye."

"And are the people still the same?" Emilie wondered.

"I believe that ye would think so." Edna had cared for many people across the last few hundred years and though much had changed, there were certain things that held true no matter the year on the calendar. "They dress differently and speak differently, but fundamentally they are the same. They laugh, they cry, they love."

"I would like to see your time."

This surprised Edna, but she realized it could be the solution to their problem. "I could arrange that if ye really mean it."

"I don't know. I cannot leave my father behind. He is alone. I am his only child," Emilie explained.

"I see. Family is important. Ye must stay for him." Separating someone from their family was never something Edna wanted to do. At times it was necessary, but in her mind only as a last resort.

"Someday?" Emilie asked.

"When I go back to me own time, it may no' be possible any longer for ye."

Emilie seemed disappointed, but asked. "Have you ever sent someone to the future from this time."

"No' from this year, but I have sent men and women through time on more than one occasion."

"Were they afraid?" Emilie's eyes went wide with curiosity.

"Perhaps at first, but they always traveled for love and that made their journey easier."

Emilie made small noises of acknowledgment, seeming satisfied with Edna's answers.

"Shall we get ye back to the palace?" Edna asked.

A resigned sigh escaped Emilie's lips. "I imagine so."

It was difficult for Edna to see Emilie's sadness at having to live the life she'd been thrust into. As with all the young ladies she'd helped, Edna's maternal instincts were strong. She had always felt protective of those she took under her wing and it was to Emilie's benefit to have Edna in her camp.

The walk back to the palace was a quiet one. Emilie would occasionally glance Edna's way and a fleeting smile would appear. This only hardened Edna's resolve. She had to make this work, not just for Emilie and Robert, but for her own standing with the council. What would they think if she came back a failure?

"LADY EDNA, come walk with me in the garden." Marie de Medici rose from her throne as Emilie and Edna entered the room. Her ladies were quick to take command of the elaborate skirt of her gown, making sure it was laid out behind her. Two of them followed along behind with the sole purpose of keeping Marie's skirt under control.

"Of course." Edna joined her as they left Emilie behind and ventured out into the beautiful garden. There was no help for Edna as her heavy skirt dragged along the ground leaving a trail in the gravel-covered walk. Her outing with Emilie had been taxing enough with the layers of clothing she was unaccustomed to wearing. She was hot and more walking was the last thing she wanted to do.

"How was your walk with Emilie?" Marie asked.

"Verra nice. I enjoyed speaking with her. She is a lovely young lass."

"I agree and so does Comte Barbieri." Marie stopped to smell a beautiful white rose along the path.

"How old is he?" Edna asked.

"Do you think he is too old for Emilie?" Marie's tone indicated disapproval of Edna's question.

Edna was unfamiliar with the rules of speaking with a royal, but she knew that Marie had a reputation for being mercurial and understood that going too far might get her banned from court. She couldn't afford that and so she proceeded with caution. "No' at all. It's just that Emilie is so young. Ye ken how young women are about love and romance. I'm sure she will be sad to lose a chance at real love."

"True love only leads to heartache. Emilie has told me of her love for Robert MacMillan. He is a soldier. A marriage between them simply would not do. I would send him away from court to save her from her longings for him, but my son is quite attached to him."

"Wouldnae it be wonderful if we were allowed to marry for love?" Edna asked, curious to hear Marie's thoughts on the subject.

"Marriage is a business arrangement. It isn't about love." Marie looked pointedly at Edna. "Emilie is the daughter of a Comte, so Barbieri is the ideal match for her."

Edna had no reply that would not anger Marie. It seemed the topic was no longer open for discussion... if it ever had been. "Yer garden is glorious today."

This topic seemed to please Marie. "The sunshine and warmth bring it happiness."

"It does the same for me." Edna chuckled and was pleased when Marie joined her.

"I hear it is often cold in Scotland," Marie said.

"I'm accustomed to it, but it is nice to be here enjoying the pleasant weather." The warm days and cooler evenings were perfect in Edna's mind.

"You are from Edinburgh?"

"Aye. We wished to be close to the king when he is at the castle," Edna lied.

"What is he like?" Marie asked.

Edna hadn't been expecting that question. She was going to have to come up with an answer that would appease Marie. "He is the king, what more can I say."

Marie wasn't listening anymore. She'd spied Concino Concini across the garden and beckoned him to join them.

"Madame Campbell," he said in greeting.

"Sir." Edna wasn't sure she wanted to continue walking with them, but Marie made that easy for her.

"It was enlightening speaking with you, Lady Edna." And she was off with Concini, leaving Edna where she stood. Once they were out of earshot, Edna couldn't help but chuckle. She had no idea why Marie had wanted to walk with her and realized perhaps there had been a different reason all along. She thought she'd wanted to talk about Emilie, but that conversation ended as quickly as it began, and Edna realized she had just been a pawn in Marie's plan to meet with Concini privately in the garden.

Edna sat on a stone bench. Her feet ached from the less-than comfortable shoes she was being forced to wear, and the corset Angus had expertly tightened was leaving little room for her to take in a deep breath. She couldn't wait to get back to her room at the inn, but for a moment she would sit and attempt to refresh herself. She relished the soft breeze rustling through the nearby trees and bushes. Birds roused from their rest among the branches and leaves complained loudly as they burst from their hiding places to take flight. A pair of doves landed on the path in front of her and ignoring Edna, pecked the ground here and there. They never wandered far from each other and their presence here on the path was symbolic to Edna. It was a representation of everlasting love. It was the love she wished for Emilie and Robert.

CHAPTER

# SIX

In his search for Edna, Angus spied Robert rushing out of the palace with purpose. He thought he should follow him and see where he was going in such a hurry. Angus was about to round the bend that would lead him out of the courtyard, through the gates and out to the road, but was stopped in his tracks by the sight of Robert and Emilie, locked in a passionate kiss and barely hidden behind some leafy trees. Young love would not be denied, but it could be brought to a sudden halt if they were not careful.

"Lord Campbell," Matteo Barbieri approached him from behind.

"Matteo," Angus said, turning quickly and blocking his path forward. "How are ye this fine day?"

"I saw you hurrying this way. Is something wrong?" Barbieri asked.

"Nae. No' at all. I was trying to find me wife. Have ye seen her?" Angus asked, hoping to keep Barbieri from heading any further toward Emilie and Robert.

"She was in the garden with Marie not long ago."

"I thought she may have gone back to the inn without telling me," Angus chuckled.

"Is this what I have to look forward to when I wed?" Matteo asked.

"Emilie seems to be a verra sweet young lass. I doubt she will cause ye any worry at all." *As long as you don't peek around the corner.* "Where were ye going when ye saw me?"

"I had no destination in mind. I thought perhaps I'd join you."

"I'm no' going anywhere either now that I ken where Edna is." He had to keep Barbieri from going through that gate. "Should we join them in the garden?" Turning him by the elbow, he searched for a subject to talk about. "Are ye feeling any better about yer upcoming marriage?"

Thankfully they were now walking away from the gate and the sight that would surely cause all hell to break loose at the palace if Barbieri had continued on that route.

"Yes. The more I think about it, the more I realize Mademoiselle Toussaint will bring with her a dowry that will add to my own wealth. It is the only reason I can see for this marriage to proceed."

"Yer quite the romantic," Angus muttered under his breath.

"I'm sorry. I did not hear what you said." Matteo leaned in closer in an apparent effort to hear better.

"It was no' important, sir. I only wished ye much happiness."

"Thank you. I'm not sure how much happiness a wife will bring, but as long as it does not cause me misery, all will be well." He laughed as he patted Angus on the back.

Angus couldn't believe what a pinchpenny Matteo was. Poor Emilie. He hoped Edna would be successful in changing her fate.

"Robert, I had to see you." Emilie rested her head on Robert's chest and relaxed into the warmth of his body. His arms held her close. She'd sent him an urgent message to meet her under the trees beyond the palace gate. Emilie knew it was risky, but after her conversation with Edna she was bubbling with hope and she wished to share it with him. Seeing Robert and feeling herself pressed so close to the muscular strength of his chest and arms was selfish of her, but she couldn't help herself. This small pleasure would sustain her as she waited for Edna to make her wish a reality.

"I thought ye were in danger," Robert replied as he stroked her hair.

"I'm sorry. I didn't mean to worry you, but would you have come otherwise?" Her fingers toyed with the edges of his shirt collar.

"Nae. I love ye, Emilie. Me heart is torn to pieces each time I see ye. To hold ye like this, to kiss yer lips... I cannae do this again. Each time we're together it only makes me want ye more, but I cannae have ye. Ye belong to another man and I must accept that we will no' be together."

"I belong to no one." Emilie was defiant, raising her voice to make her point. "I will not marry Barbieri. Madame Campbell will help me. She has told me so."

He shook his head. "Nae one can help us. The Queen Mother has made up her mind, as has yer da. If I could change the outcome, I would." He took her face in his hands, gazing into her eyes. "Ye are the only woman for me, ye ken it. I wish for nae other."

"Why do you say we cannot be helped? You will see. We will be together. For now, I must continue to go along with the marriage plans, but there will be no marriage in the end. I know it." She was confident her wish upon the moon had made it so.

"Madame Campbell is Angus' wife, is she no'?" Robert asked.

Emilie nodded.

"She shouldnae lie to ye as she has." He sounded angry.

"She's not lying." Emilie felt the need to defend the woman who would end this nightmare she was living. "I made a wish on the moon and Edna arrived to help me." Leaning back, Emilie looked up at him. "Robert, what if we could run away to a time and a place far from here. Would you go with me?"

"If I thought it would do us any good, I would. They would search for ye and when we were found they would bring us back here. Living life on the run is no' the life for ye. Ye deserve so much more." Robert caressed Emilie's cheek with his hand. "Me love. Hope is wasted where we are concerned. We must end these meetings."

Emilie couldn't believe what he was saying. It hurt her heart to hear his words. "Don't speak to me of love. If you would dismiss me so easily, you cannot have loved me from the beginning." Blinded by tears, Emilie pushed his arms away and ran as fast as she could back to her room where she sobbed into her pillows and wished she hadn't said the things she did. She knew Robert loved her, but Emilie couldn't understand why he would give up so easily. He didn't believe that her wish on the moon had brought Edna to help them. If she hadn't experienced it herself, perhaps she might not believe it either. How much longer could she go on with this charade? If Emilie wanted to have her love in the end, she would have to continue with it. What other choice was there?

THE PAIN in Robert's chest was beyond anything he'd ever experienced in his life. He wondered if this was what a broken heart felt like? He had no wish to hurt Emilie, but he couldn't understand why she persisted in believing that they would ever be together. Love wasn't in the cards for them, and yet he couldn't stop himself from loving her. That was the cause of his pain. It was a pain he would carry throughout his life without her.

Retrieving his horse from the stable, Robert was about to ride out on his own when Louis arrived.

"Robert, where are you off to?" Louis asked, motioning to his servants to prepare his horse.

"I need to get away. I need time to think." He was about to ride off, but Louis continued speaking to him.

"You won't mind if I join you then." He gestured to the stable boys nearby and they jumped into action.

He couldn't tell Louis he wanted to be alone and did not wish his company. That was something one did not say to a king and so he said, "Of course no'."

Within just a few minutes, the horse had been saddled and was brought to the king. "Is something bothering you?" Louis mounted his steed. "Wait. Don't tell me until we are on our way. Where are we going?"

"I was going to ride along the river banks," Robert said.

Robert's horse began to walk and Louis caught up to ride by his side. "Tell me what troubles you."

It was a command. Robert didn't mind talking to Louis about what was on his mind. The lad was rather knowledgeable, for being only ten and three. That was a good thing because soon he would take over the reign of the kingdom from his mother.

"Is it Emilie?" Louis asked.

"Aye. She refuses to believe that we cannae be together," Robert admitted.

"I refuse to believe that as well." Louis sounded indignant for his friend.

"What do ye ken about love, Louis? Have ye ever been in love?" Robert couldn't believe he should be taking advice from Louis on romance.

"No, I have not and I don't know much about love, but I do know that when you look at Emilie, I can see something different there. Robert the warrior and Robert my guard vanish to be replaced by a much softer man." It was quite an observation for one so young.

"I doona believe that to be true."

"I am wise beyond my years, as you often tell me. I am not questioning your strength. I know what I see. I also know that she looks at you the same way. Anyone else present disappears from view when you have this look."

Robert didn't speak. Louis was right. He hadn't been doing a very good job of hiding his feelings.

"I will speak to my mother." Louis' nose tipped upwards showing the pride he felt in helping Robert. "She will listen to me."

"Please doona." Robert was exasperated by this whole issue. He wanted it all to be over and he feared that speaking to the Queen Mother would only cause trouble for Emilie.

Louis dropped his head and wrinkling his brow, turned to look at Robert. "Why? It cannot hurt to let her know that she is breaking the heart of someone who is very important to me."

"I cannae stop you, but ye willnae change her mind. I am sure of it." It was impossible to argue with Louis when he'd made up his mind about something. There was simply no point to it now.

"You must continue meeting with Emilie. I prefer a happy Robert to the sullen Robert I am riding with."

"Seeing Emilie is what caused this mood and was the reason for this ride."

Louis seemed to be mulling this over and for a while they rode in silence.

"Shall we race to the trees up ahead near the bend in the river?" Louis asked. An impish grin spread across his face and before Robert could answer, the lad moved his horse into a fluid canter and then a gallop. Louis' long, curly hair flowed freely out behind him as he urged his horse to move faster.

Robert could catch and pass him, but it wasn't a good idea to beat the king at anything. Louis expected to win and Robert would let him. However, he needed to at least catch up with him so the lad believed he won fairly and also so that he could ensure Louis' safety.

He squeezed his legs and pushed his horse forward to a gallop, holding him back just enough so he would not pass Louis.

Louis reached the bend in the river just ahead of Robert. He whooped loudly, declaring victory. Robert couldn't help but chuckle. "Ye win once again Louis. Will I ever be able to beat ye?"

"If you give your horse his head and allow him to run as he wishes, you just might."

"Next time." Robert turned his horse back towards the palace and Louis joined him, riding up beside him.

"I enjoy nothing more than riding fast. It is thrilling don't you agree?" Louis leaned forward to pat his horse's neck as he praised him for his beauty, strength and speed.

"It frees the mind of any and all thought."

Louis tipped his head as he gazed at Robert. "You are right. It does."

Edna watched as Angus stoked the fire in the hearth. The weather had been warm during the days they'd been in Paris, but the evening air had a chill that permeated their room.

"How was yer day?" Edna asked.

"Informative." Angus poked at an errant log, pushing it into place next to the others and holding it there until it caught fire.

"How so?" Edna placed her cape on the edge of the bed.

Angus moved away from the fire and sat on the bed. "I happened to see Robert and Emilie together."

"Oh." Edna's brow furrowed with concern. If Marie found out about this she would be angry, and it was well known that she could be unpredictable.

"If they had been seen it would have been a disaster," Angus said, echoing Edna's thoughts.

"So true. I will have to speak with Emilie about that."

"Especially since Matteo was headed straight towards them. If I hadnae been there, he would have seen them together."

"So ye distracted him." Edna was relieved.

"I did. He wanted the company, so I walked with him and he spoke to me about the betrothal."

The pause in the conversation went on a little longer than Edna liked. She wasn't sure Angus planned to continue and her impatience was showing. "Well, are ye going to tell me what he said?"

"Sorry, love. I was just thinking. Unfortunately, it seems he's warming to the idea of marriage to Emilie. He's looking forward to adding her dowry to his coffers."

"So it's the money he's interested in," Edna said, feeling somewhat vindicated. She knew there had to be a reason Matteo had agreed to this marriage.

"It's certainly no' Emilie. If he could have the money without the wife, he'd happily take it," Angus confirmed.

"If only we had enough money to give him so he'd go back home without her," Edna grumbled. "Short of that, I would have to use me magic, but getting Matteo alone could be a challenge and ye ken that it could be dangerous for us if I was found out."

"Ye must be careful, but how can we overcome the situation without it?" Angus wondered.

"I doona ken. I'm trying to understand the motivations of all those involved and it's no' looking good." Edna stood in front of the fire, feeling a sudden chill. "I spoke with Marie today and she is adamant about the wedding for all the reasons that we've learned." She rattled off the list, using her fingers to address each one. "Robert is a soldier. He's no' in the same social caste. Marriage is a business contract. Nae love necessary. She really has nae care for the fact that Emilie is a young woman who needs to be loved and Matteo is an old man who, as ye learned today, only cares about what Emilie's dowry will bring to the marriage. It's infuriating."

"I can see the steam coming from yer ears," Angus chuckled.

"It's no' funny, Angus. How am I to do what I came here for if I get nae cooperation from the powers that be?" She turned to look at him, throwing her arms in the air in frustration.

"Come here, me love." Angus held his arms out to her. "Perhaps a night in the arms of the man who adores ye above all else will help."

Edna happily went to him and was immediately engulfed in his embrace. They shared slow, intense kisses, each one becoming more and more fiery.

Angus pulled Edna down on the bed next to him. "Tomorrow we'll solve the problems of the world. Tonight is ours."

Edna needed no coaxing. She cleared her mind and allowed Angus to work his magic.

CHAPTER

# SEVEN

At court the next morning, Edna sought out Emilie, who was with Marie and the other ladies-of-the-court.

"May we have a word?" Edna whispered to her, tapping her on the shoulder.

Emilie acknowledged Edna and then looked to Marie who was busy with her dressmaker. She nodded and followed Edna out of the room. "What is it?"

They walked down a long ornate corridor with high ceilings and painted murals, but Edna was too concerned about Emilie to admire any of the beautiful things they passed.

"I hear ye met with Robert yesterday," Edna said.

"I did." Emilie's mood was hard to decipher. She didn't have the usual lilt to her voice when Robert was the topic. "How did you know?"

"I have me ways. It dinna go well, did it?" Edna asked.

"No. He told me we have no future. That we should not meet again." Emilie seemed a mixture of sad, angry and resigned as she spoke.

"I see." Edna was going to tell her the same thing, but Robert had beaten her to it. "Ye were almost caught. Angus stopped Matteo before he stumbled upon the two of ye."

"I wish he had caught us. Then maybe he wouldn't wish to marry me."

"It wouldnae be good for yer reputation and he would still wish to marry ye because he is interested in yer dowry, which I'm sure he has discussed with Marie and yer father."

Emilie stopped and faced Edna. "Matteo has not spoken to my father. Marie was the one who arranged things with him."

"Truly?" Edna asked as they began walking again.

"My father has been ill and not taking visitors. When he is well again they will meet."

"When was the last time ye saw yer father?" Edna asked.

"He came to the palace a month ago to speak with the Queen Mother about the betrothal. I had no idea. I thought he was just here to visit with me as he has in the past. Her Highness does not like me to leave the court and so it has been years since I've been home. When he told me he had approved the marriage I became upset and left before he could say another thing. I haven't seen him since."

"Well, we must remedy that. It is nae good for ye to go without seeing him. He may be the only one other than me who can help."

Emilie stopped once again and turned toward Edna. "If you have witch powers to help me, why haven't you?" There was a note of accusation in her voice.

"Me plan *is* to help ye, but I would like to assess the situation fully before I use me powers. It could be quite dangerous for me, just as it was for Madame DuBois to give ye the stone ye used to wish on the moon. Ye understand that, doona ye?"

Emilie nodded, her eyes cast downward.

Edna gave her hand a squeeze of encouragement. She understood that this was difficult and wanted her to know that she was on her side.

"I'm sorry. I'm impatient and afraid that it won't work and I'll be married to Matteo and on my way to Italy before anything can be done to stop it. I'll never see Robert again."

"Me dear, I understand yer fear and impatience so I ask ye to stay away from Robert for the time being. If ye see him across the room, look away. Nae one can ken that ye are still in love with him." Edna took her arm. "Ye will be together soon enough. Ye must trust me."

"What if he stops loving me?" Emilie asked. Her voice shook. It was obvious she was on the verge of tears.

Edna turned to her and lifted Emilie's chin with her hand. "Havenae ye heard the saying, absence makes the heart grow fonder?" It was completely possible that the saying hadn't been used in this time period and that Emilie hadn't heard it before based on the blank look on her face. "Robert loves ye now and he will always love ye. I promise." It was a promise she intended to keep. She was Edna Campbell and she knew love when she saw it. "Now, put a smile on that pretty face of yers and never let them see ye looking sad like this again."

Emilie's smile was half-hearted, but Edna thought it was good enough to fool anyone who didn't really care enough to know her feelings. Unfortunately, that included Marie and Matteo.

ANGUS HAPPENED to be nearby as Louis approached his mother. He was close enough to hear their conversation without them noticing and didn't feel the least bit guilty about eavesdropping. They nodded as they walked past him and down the center aisle of the garden. Angus followed behind them, examining flowers and hedges as though he had a keen interest in botany.

"Mother, I am concerned about my guard Robert. He is so obviously in love with Emilie Toussaint and she with him. You must not force her to marry Barbieri."

"It's of no concern to you," Marie answered.

"Why wouldn't it be? If you were no longer regent, I would be making these decisions."

"That is true, but you are not and so it is up to me to choose a husband for Emilie." Marie looked away from Louis for a moment, seeming to examine the garden.

"It is not necessary that you do so," Louis said.

"No. However it is something I wish to do and as you will soon find when you are king, we can do whatever we want without disagreement from anyone. Besides, I have my reasons. Emilie needs a husband and Concini suggested Barbieri."

"I do not care for Concini. Why does he care who Emilie Toussaint marries?"

"He merely made a suggestion and I agreed it would be a good match. Emilie's father wished for her to marry. He is ill and it was important for him to see her wed to a man who would take care of her. Robert MacMillan is not that man."

"She does not love Barbieri."

"Of course not. You are young, my son, and unaware of the sacrifices women must make in this world."

"I will be old enough to be king soon enough and I understand the ways of the court better than you think."

Angus moved a bit closer. He could see Louis was becoming angry, but Marie was obviously not bothered. In fact, she seemed rather dismissive of her son's concerns.

"Until the day that you take the throne and no longer need me, I will continue to act as regent. No argument you may have will change my mind." She paused for a moment, seeming to think. "I have been thinking it might be best to send Robert back to Scotland and get you a new guard."

Louis erupted on hearing this. "You wouldn't dare. I will not allow it."

"Then I suggest you understand that nothing you can say or do will change matters."

Louis turned and spun away, charging past Angus. An angry

scowl on his face spoke of the tumultuous relationship he had with his mother. Angus continued staring at the green leaves in front of him as though he really cared about what he was seeing.

"You there," Marie called to him. "You are Edna Campbell's husband, are you not?"

Angus bowed his head to Marie. "Angus Campbell, Yer Highness."

"Do you have a son?" Marie looked quite perturbed as she stared past him at Louis' retreating back.

"We have been blessed with a daughter, but nae, we do no' have a son."

"Consider yourself lucky then," Marie huffed.

"They may no' be sons, but in addition to our daughter, me wife has taken many a young lady into her heart, treating each of them as if they were her own. She can tell ye that even without that familial connection they doona always understand that we are only doing what we feel is best for them."

"Hmmm... they can be most ungrateful as well." She pursed her lips, accentuating the frown that wrinkled her brow.

Not sure what to say at this point, Angus said the only thing a polite gentleman should say. "Is there anything I can do to help?"

"Not unless you can get Robert MacMillan to go home." She pulled a fan from the sleeve of her gown and waved it back and forth in front of her reddened face.

Angus realized that this could change everything and not for the better. "He is devoted to yer son. He wouldnae wish to leave his post, I am sure."

"Yes. Well, he may have to. Good day to you, sir." Marie marched off to the palace, leaving Angus standing there with plant material still in his hands.

Angus would have much to share with Edna when they met a little later on. For now, he would enjoy the fair weather and a good walk. Hopefully he wouldn't run into anyone else who had anything to do with Edna's mission here, but it seemed that wasn't going to be the case.

"Angus I must speak with ye." Robert MacMillan strode towards him like a man on a mission.

"Aye. What is it?" Angus spun the flower he now held in his hands.

"Yer wife." Robert's voice rose in apparent anger.

"What about her?" Angus asked, using his hands to tell Robert to bring his voice down.

"She's telling lies to Emilie," Robert's voice was gruff with emotion.

"I'm no' sure what ye mean," Angus said. He wasn't sure what Edna had done this time, but he was sure she wasn't lying.

"She has Emilie believing some fairytale about the moon and love and that we'll be together. It's a lie and ye must ken it." Robert was barely controlling himself.

Angus wasn't sure he should be sharing this information with Robert, but he could see the pain the man carried with him.

"Tell me what has happened." Angus kept his voice low and his demeanor calm.

"I told Emilie we cannae see each other again. She was angry and upset with me." His chest heaved up and down as he spoke.

"And she told ye about Edna." Angus didn't like this. If he didn't share with Robert there was every chance Robert would say something to Louis and then Edna would be accused of witchcraft. But if he did tell him, the same may be true.

"Aye. She did."

"Robert, I'll share something with ye, but ye must promise me on yer honor that ye willnae tell a soul. Can I count on ye?" He looked him directly in the eye.

"Of course. I'll no' say a word."

Angus took in a deep breath and letting it go, knew what he had to do. "This is going to sound unbelievable, but Edna and I are from a different time, in the future. Emilie made a wish on the moon and we were tasked with coming here to help make that wish come true."

Robert's eyes narrowed as he furrowed his brow. Angus waited for him to fully understand what he'd just said before he would continue.

"Is it true?" Robert backed away from him. A brief flash of fear appeared on his face. He took a moment, eyeing Angus the whole time.

Angus waited, hoping Robert would make the decision to believe him. If he didn't, it could spell disaster for all of them. It took a few moments, but the fear faded from his face, replaced with curiosity and just a bit of hope. "Doona be afraid. It is true. It is why we are here. Now, do ye trust me and can I trust ye to keep this secret?"

"Aye. 'Tis the strangest story I've ever heard. I trust that ye would no' lie to me."

"Good. Now 'tis best for all involved to let Edna do her work. She will try to fix this first without using magic, but if she can no' it will be employed."

Robert's confusion was obvious as his brows scrunched and his eye twitched. "Why would she do this for us? I doona understand."

Angus hurried to alleviate Robert's discomfiture. "If ye ken anything at all about me wife, ye'd ken that she will do anything for love. She has matched many couples over the years and now it is yer turn."

A relieved smile broke out on Robert's face. "I *almost* believe ye and I am grateful for the help. Is there anything I must do?"

"I believe it would be best to stay away from each other. We doona need to raise suspicion at this point. Ye are lucky ye were no' caught today."

"It will be difficult to do, but I ken meeting her today put us both in danger. It willnae happen again." Robert looked up at the sky, as if he were looking for answers. Then shaking his head in disbelief asked, "Yer wife is a witch?"

"Shhh… Doona speak of it." Angus glanced around to make sure no one was nearby.

Robert held his hands up in what seemed an effort to calm Angus. "Sorry. I'll no' say it again."

"Thank ye. I'm no' sure I was to tell ye what I did. Edna may be angry with me."

"I pray she is no'. Ye are a good man and have only done what was necessary."

"I think so and ye think so, but Edna may have had other plans." He thought he had information to share with her before, but this information would be vital. "Doona worry. Go about yer day. All will be well."

"Thank ye for yer honesty, Angus. I will tell nae one." He smiled again. "My heart is lighter now and the pain has left me."

Angus watched as he walked away. He was happy to have given him hope. Now it was up to Edna to fulfill their dreams of being together.

THAT NIGHT there was another reception at the palace. This time it was for some traveling dignitaries who'd arrived from Rome. Edna and Angus had been invited to attend. In the short time they'd been at Tuileries, they'd become a part of the court, which Edna was grateful for. Being close to Emilie and Robert made her job a little easier. She'd forgiven Angus for telling Robert, even though she wasn't actually angry with him. It had been perfectly all right for him to do so. She might have even done it herself sooner or later.

The ballroom was brightly lit by chandeliers glowing with candles high above their heads and tall candelabra set about the room. Experiencing history in this way was so much better than reading about it in books.

Concino Concini seemed to be well acquainted with the evening's special guests. He paraded them around the room introducing them to the comtes, viscomtes, dukes and barons who were in attendance. He bypassed Edna and Angus, which was not surprising. It was clear since their arrival that he looked on them as his inferiors and felt no need to be bothered even speaking with them. Edna's intuition told her he was up to no good. She got an uncomfortable feeling every time he was around. From what she'd witnessed, he seemed to delight in causing trouble. Being Marie's favorite elevated him in the eyes of almost everyone at court and so he seemed to always let it be known that he was quite important. Yes, he was up to something and Edna was determined to find out what.

"Good evening," Matteo Barbieri greeted them. Unlike Concini he appeared to enjoy Angus' company and made a point of chatting with him whenever he saw him.

"Good evening, Matteo. Are ye enjoying yerself?" Angus asked.

He made a face that bordered on a mixture of irritation and disgust. "I don't enjoy these receptions, but I will do my best to seem pleased to be here."

"Ye're doing a verra good job," Edna said.

"Madame Campbell. It is a pleasure to see you." Matteo bowed slightly in her direction.

"And ye," she replied. "Where is Emilie?"

"She wasn't feeling well, so she has stayed in her room. I imagine she did not relish this event any more than I do."

"Do ye ken the visitors?" Angus asked.

Matteo looked toward the visitors. "No. They are friends of Concini."

"I thought ye were friends with Concini. Is that no' the case?" Edna couldn't be sure, but it seemed Barbieri wasn't happy with his friend for some reason.

"Concini brought me here under false pretenses. Once I arrived, I found that it was the Queen Mother's wish that I marry Emilie."

"And ye agreed?" Edna wanted to get to the bottom of this.

"The Medici's are a powerful family. It is best not to cross them. I have business in Rome and without their blessing I would find it difficult to continue my business there."

The energy of the room changed as the music came to an abrupt ending and the large doors on the far end of the room opened. The young king entered the room with his entourage, which included Robert. Everyone turned towards him, bowing as he passed them on his way to his mother's side. Once there, he waved his hand and the music started up once again. The lad knew how to make a grand entrance.

Edna admired those who were dancing. Pretty and colorful gowns swirled around the room in shades of pink, green, orange and blue.

"You do not dance?" Barbieri said, noticing her interest in those who were.

"Oh, nae. Unfortunately, I have turned me ankle and should no'." She couldn't say she didn't know these dances. Every woman of this time worth her salt knew them.

Looking down towards her feet, Matteo didn't seem as though he believed her. "I'm sorry to hear that. I'm sure you would enjoy being out there with everyone. The music makes us all happy."

"I believe it does," she replied.

"What of you Angus?" Matteo asked.

"What about me?" Angus asked.

"Do you enjoy the music?"

"Verra much. I must admit I doona care to dance though."

"If Emilie were here, I would have a dance partner. Instead I will be satisfied to watch."

"Emilie tells me ye havenae met her father yet." Edna was curious to know how he felt about that.

"He has been ill. If I do not meet him, so be it. It is not necessary, though it would be proper."

"I imagine so." Edna elbowed Angus. It didn't seem that Barbieri was all that interested in speaking with her and Angus was being too quiet for her liking.

"How long has he been ill?" Angus asked, apparently getting the hint.

"I don't know. He has been ill since I've been here at court." Matteo watched the couples dancing past them with an apparent wish to join them, despite his age.

"I pray he's better soon then," Angus said. "I'm sure Emilie will want him at her wedding."

The music paused momentarily and an awkward silence ensued among the three of them. It was obvious Barbieri didn't care one way or the other. The betrothal was nothing more than a means to an end. He no more wanted to marry Emilie than she wanted to marry him, but he had more reason to go through with it than she did.

"Where in Italy are ye from, Matteo?" Angus asked.

"Rome, of course." His chest puffed out with pride as he spoke.

"It is a beautiful city," Edna said.

"You've been?" Matteo sounded hopeful.

"Nae. I've heard," she replied.

"You must come to visit us." The invitation was cordial and seemed sincere. "Once we are married we will leave right away. I have business to attend to and I've been away too long."

"When is the wedding?" Edna hadn't been too worried about that, but it seemed Matteo was already making plans to head home.

"In one week's time," he replied.

"So soon," Edna said. It was a lot sooner than she'd originally thought.

"Not so soon. As I've said I have business to attend to. If I stay here much longer it will be a disaster."

Edna snuck a peek at Angus, who raised his eyebrows in surprise.

"If you'll excuse me. I must speak with Her Highness," Matteo said.

"Of course." Edna watched him walk away and once he was out of earshot, grabbed Angus by the arm and steered him towards the doors to the garden. "Angus, we doona have as much time as I thought. We've got to get Emilie to visit her father. Perhaps I can talk some sense into him."

"Agreed. She's no' here tonight. Ye'll have to speak with her in the morning."

"We'll need to make arrangements right away."

"I'm always at the ready," Angus said with a wink.

Edna couldn't help but laugh. "Stop being such a tease."

"I wish we knew how to do these fancy dances. I'd love to take ye for a whirl around the dance floor."

Angus looked at Edna with such a sweet look of disappointment that she almost wanted to give the dances a try, but then thought better of it. "We doona want to embarrass ourselves now, do we?"

Angus snorted out a laugh.

Edna giggled on hearing it. "We can embarrass ourselves in our room at the inn with our own music and our own dance."

"How much longer do we have to stay?" Angus asked sounding eager to be on their way.

"We can go any time ye like."

He held his arm out for Edna. "Now would be good."

"And we'll dance when we get there?" Edna teased.

Angus pulled her close. "Do ye even need to ask?"

# CHAPTER
# EIGHT

"Ye dinna tell me the wedding was to be in a week," Edna said to Emilie. They stood in the courtyard outside of the palace doors.

"I'm sorry. I didn't know the date had changed. Marie told me last night before the reception."

"Is that why ye dinna attend?" Edna was concerned for Emilie's health. She was looking quite pale this morning.

"Yes. Matteo wants to get back home and he doesn't want to wait for my father to be able to attend the wedding."

Edna knew it was time to take action. She'd thought there would be more time, but things had changed and now they had a deadline that was swiftly approaching. "Me dear, we must visit yer father right away."

"I know." Emilie twisted the edges of her cloak between her fingers. Her anxiety was apparent to anyone who took the time to notice. "I was so angry when I last saw him. I must apologize for my behavior. I hope he will forgive me." Sadness and devastation flowed from her words and through her appearance.

Edna took her hand, patting it gently as she spoke. "He loves ye,

Emilie. I'm sure he'll forgive ye. Angus and I will escort ye today. It is important that we see him right away. We'll arrange for a carriage. If we're lucky it will be here shortly."

"I must tell Marie and pack a few things. It will only take a moment." She hurried back inside while Edna waited and Angus went in search of a carriage.

Angus must have been lucky, because a carriage soon drew up in front of the doors. The driver hopped down and opened the door to the carriage. Angus hopped out.

"That was fast," Edna said.

"Where's Emilie?" Angus asked, glancing around the courtyard.

"She'll be right back. She had to tell Marie we were going." Edna looked anxiously to the doors of the palace.

"I'm here," Emilie called as she hurried towards them with what looked like a large purse in her hand.

"Tell the driver where we'll be going, dear." Edna said.

Emilie gave the driver instructions while Edna waited. Angus held the door open for both ladies and helped them inside. Emilie sat by the window on the far side of the carriage while Edna and Angus sat together opposite her.

"I told the driver to hurry as much as he possibly could. We will have to stay the night with my father. It takes hours to get there by carriage. It will be dark before we arrive." Emilie dabbed at her nose with a handkerchief as she turned to look out the window trying to hide her emotional state from Edna and Angus.

Understanding her state, Edna decided to focus on something else in the hopes it would take Emilie's mind off of her father and her impending marriage, at least for a moment or two. "I sometimes forget how long it takes to go places in this time."

"Is it faster in the future?" Emilie seemed to perk up as she turned towards Edna. Her curiosity was evident every time Edna mentioned the future.

"Much faster," Angus answered. "In the future it might only take us one hour to get there."

"Oh how I wish we were in the future. I would like to be with my father this very moment." Emilie went back to gazing out the window of the carriage, while Edna exchanged a worried look with Angus.

They passed through the beautiful French countryside along the way, though no one was particularly interested in the scenery. After a stop for food and a rest break, it was quite dark when they arrived at the house and were greeted by Comte Toussaint's footman.

"Mademoiselle Toussaint, I am so happy you have arrived," the man said.

"Is my father able to take visitors?" The worry in her voice was evident.

The man sent a sad look to Edna and Angus before speaking directly to Emilie. "His condition has worsened. The doctor is with him now, but there is nothing he can do. It happened so fast."

Tears immediately formed in Emilie's eyes. Edna couldn't bear to see her in such pain and so she wrapped her arms around her, holding her close and whispering in her ear. "I'm so sorry, Emilie."

Edna and Angus escorted her inside. The Toussaint home was large and from the outside, very impressive. Once inside, though, it was clear that it was in need of repair. The furniture, curtains and rugs were worn with age, the walls were a mess of peeling paint and paper. Something was definitely amiss.

Edna exchanged a questioning glance with Angus. "We'll wait for ye here while ye speak with yer father."

"Claude, please show our guests to the salon." Emilie seemed to shudder as she took in a deep breath and headed up the stairs to see her father.

THE CURTAINS HAD BEEN DRAWN and the room was dark. Emilie peered toward her father's bed and was shocked at the sight that met her gaze. Even in the dimly lit room it was evident how ill he was. Guilt and anguish over her lack of communication with him set in. If only she'd listened to him and not argued, perhaps she would have spent more time with him. What difference would it have made to her if she'd merely accepted what he'd told her instead of arguing and storming off? All of her quarreling made not one bit of difference in the end. She had lost what little time was left with her father and was still being forced to marry Matteo, that was the truth of it. She moved closer to the bed, holding her breath and holding back her tears.

"Father?" Her voice shook with the fear overtaking her.

"Emilie? Is that you?" Florimond Toussaint's voice was weak and seemed far away.

He turned his head toward her and as his eyes met hers, Emilie rushed to his side. The doctor was packing his bag and preparing to leave. "How is he, doctor?"

"He will not last much longer." His words were spoken softly as though he feared she might break on hearing them. "It is good that you are here."

"Emilie, sit with me." Florimond's hand beckoned her to come closer.

She sat on the edge of the bed, taking his hand into hers and realizing, perhaps for the first time, how much she loved those hands. They had held her as a baby, taken her hand as he walked with her when she was a small child and always treated her with love and kindness. His fingers were long and not as strong as they'd once been. How strange that in this moment it was the one thing she was focused on.

"Look at me," Florimond requested, his tone quiet and filled with emotion. "Emilie, I love you more than you could possibly understand. When last we parted my heart was broken. I thought I might never see you again. You were so angry with me."

"I love you, too, father. I'm sorry that I argued with you that day and even sorrier that I have stayed away for as long as I have," she fought to hold back her tears.

"I want to explain why I agreed to your betrothal." He took in a breath that seemed shallow and weak before he could continue. "I have not been good with my finances. I have made poor business decisions and trusted those who were not trustworthy." He stopped, struggling for his breath.

"I don't understand," Emilie said, touching his face with her hand.

"I have nothing left. This house and the furniture in it are no longer mine. I have only been allowed to stay because I will be gone soon. They have given me at least that one kindness."

"Who are *they*?" Emilie asked. She was frightened for her father, but did her best to remain calm so as not to upset him.

"Concino Concini has arranged to pay off my debts. I do not have the strength to explain it all. You are what is important to me. I want you to be taken care of. Comte Barbieri will do that and it is the reason I agreed to the marriage."

She could tell him once again that she didn't love the man and that she would spend her life being miserable because she was losing Robert, but she didn't want these final words between them to be filled with disagreement. "Father, did mother love you when you wed?"

"No. We were barely acquainted, but with time we grew to love each other very much. I have missed her all these years that she has been gone. I know she is waiting for me. She told me in my dreams last night."

Emilie couldn't help herself. The tears flowed like a waterfall from her eyes.

"Come here, my darling daughter." Florimond held one arm up.

Emilie nestled in beside him, resting her head on his frail shoulder. "Am I hurting you?" She worried she was.

"No. I am happy you are here with me. Will you stay?"

"I will not leave you, I promise."

∽

EDNA PACED BACK and forth across the threadbare carpet of the salon. Emilie had been gone quite some time and Edna was worried about what might be happening upstairs. The sound of footsteps told her she'd have her answer soon enough.

"He's gone." Emilie entered the room. Her eyes, puffy from crying, told the story.

"I'm so sorry, me dear." Edna went to her and wrapped her in a warm hug. Angus joined them, folding both women in his embrace.

"I'm glad I was here. I would not want him to have died alone." Emilie sniffled and wiped her nose with her hankie.

"Did ye make amends?" Edna asked.

"Yes. All was well between us when he took his final breath."

Edna could feel the weight of Emilie's body as she sagged into their arms and cried.

"I would like to stay a day or two," Emilie said through her sobs. "I must send the Queen Mother a note to explain my delay in returning to court.

"Of course. Is there anything else we can do?" Edna asked.

"I'd like to bury him beside my mother, but as I've come to find out we are quite broke. All of the servants are gone."

"I'll take care of it, lass. Perhaps Claude could join me," Angus suggested.

"I will ask."

Edna didn't wish to bring up Matteo. This wasn't the right time, but things may have just taken a turn in Emilie's favor. She would speak of it when they were making their return trip to the palace. Right now poor Emilie was in shock. She'd just lost her father and was obviously feeling the weight of being alone.

"Angus, I can help as well," Edna offered.

"Edna, would you help me prepare him for burial?" Emilie asked.

"Of course I will. Do ye need some time to rest first?" Edna was concerned that Emilie would collapse at any moment, but it was clear she was doing her best to be brave in the face of this great loss.

Edna herself felt tears welling in her own eyes as she felt Emilie's pain.

"I'd like to take care of it right away. Keeping busy is best." A small sob escaped her lips.

Edna hurried to place an arm around her waist for fear she might fall. "Shall we collect the things we will need?"

Edna walked with Emilie, holding her close as they headed to Florimond Toussaint's chambers. Her heart ached for the lass. She knew how hard it was to lose a parent. It would take time for her to get over it. "Emilie, ye will always remember yer father. He will live forever in yer heart, but with each passing day the pain of yer loss will become more bearable."

"I know. I remember what it was like when my mother passed. My father and I had each other. We were not alone." Her voice broke once again as she spoke.

"Ye are nae alone, Emilie. Angus and I are here for ye. In time all will be well." Edna knew her words, though meant to reassure Emilie, were not penetrating Emilie's grief.

In the hall at the foot of the stairs, Claude appeared. His concern on seeing Emilie was evident as he glanced from her to Edna and then to Angus who was following along behind them.

"Claude, my father is no longer with us. Will you help Lord Campbell with the burial?"

"Beside your mother, mademoiselle?" Claude asked.

"Yes. Is there anyone else here to help?" Emilie questioned.

"I'm afraid not. I am the only one who stayed." He turned to Angus. "If you'll follow me, sir."

The two men left the house together and the ladies went up the stairs to attend to Florimond.

THE CARRIAGE RIDE BACK to Tuileries was quiet. Emilie stared out the window occasionally dabbing at her eyes with her handkerchief. In her mind, her life was no longer her own. All hope had been lost and she would be at the mercy of Marie de Medici now that she was alone and penniless. Emilie could see from the concerned looks Edna shared with Angus that they were worried about her and wished there was something they could do to help.

As they neared the palace, Emilie straightened and wiped her eyes one final time. "We're back. I will tell the Queen Mother that I would like to go through with the marriage right away. There is no need to wait." She said the words that she never imagined she would say.

"Emilie, ye doona mean that," Edna said.

"I do. I am merely following my father's last wishes. He explained the reason he went through with the betrothal was only so that I would be taken care of. He felt Comte Barbieri would be the one to do that."

Edna seemed shocked and Emilie could understand why.

"I cannae let ye go through with this. If ye doona want to marry Matteo, there are ways I can use me magic to help."

"That won't be necessary. I will do what is right." Emilie straightened her spine and held her head high.

She watched Edna's face turn pale as she turned to her husband and then back to face her. Edna's voice sounded frantic to her ears. "I cannae let ye do it," Edna said again. "It's no' what ye want. What about Robert? What about love?"

"I can live without them," she lied. "I shall look forward to making a new life in Rome with Matteo."

Edna seemed as though she might jump right out of her skin as her panicked gaze fell on Emilie. "I'm no' sure what to do," she said to Angus before turning to face Emilie. "I ken in me heart, Emilie, that ye doona mean what ye are saying. I ken this is no' what ye want. I did no' travel all the way through time to fail in me mission, but I can see that now isnae a good time to talk about this. I want ye to ken that I am no' giving up on ye and Robert."

"I appreciate all you've tried to do for me, Edna, but my mind is made up. It is for the best."

As Emilie entered the throne room, Marie de Medici and Concino Concini were deep in conversation. She cleared her throat to get their attention.

"Emilie, you are back," Marie said.

She curtsied to the Queen Mother. "I have news. My father has passed away."

"I'm so sorry. I knew he was sick, but thought he would be well enough to attend your nuptials," Marie said.

Emilie noted that Concino Concini stood a little taller and seemed much more interested in what she was saying than he ever had before. He was undoubtedly happy to hear the news as a small smile lifted one corner of his lips before disappearing and being replaced with a false look of concern.

"I am happy I was able to be with him in the end. I wish to tell you that the sooner I can marry the better. It was my father's only wish for me and I will honor him."

"Of course. I will speak to Barbieri. He will be thrilled. He is very interested in going home as soon as possible."

Maintaining a serious demeanor, Emilie was determined not to let Marie see any doubt or weakness. "I will be happy to join him."

"Good. I'm glad you are no longer resisting this marriage. Remember, I always know what is best. It is why I chose him for you."

"I am grateful," Emilie said, bowing her head, doing her best not to show her disdain for Concini.

"Now, if you'll excuse us." Marie went back to her conversation with Concini.

Emilie knew when she had been dismissed. When Marie was

done speaking with you, she just pretended you were no longer there.

Wandering aimlessly out into the garden and not paying attention to where she was going, Emilie found herself at the stables just as Robert dismounted his horse. She tried to walk away, but he'd seen her.

"Emilie, are ye well?" He handed his horse to a groom and was at her side in a heartbeat. "I dinna see ye at court yesterday. Where were ye?"

"My father has died." She thought she had no more tears to cry, but somehow being in the presence of someone who truly cared about her had them flowing once again.

Robert took her in his arms. Neither of them had a care that they may be seen. He held her tight. "I'm so sorry, Emilie."

"I don't know what to do. I don't want to be alone. All I can do is think about him." She poured out her heart to Robert.

"I understand. It is normal. There is naething wrong with the way ye feel. Ye are grieving the loss of a verra important man in yer life." He rubbed her back while still holding her close.

The warmth of that embrace was exactly what she needed, but she would soon be grieving the loss of not just her father. She would be losing Robert as well. Her heart was breaking, but she had to tell him, knowing that even as she did she would not feel that warm embrace ever again. It took everything she had in her to say the words she was about to say. "I must marry Matteo as soon as it can be arranged. It was my father's final wish. We will leave for Rome immediately after the ceremony."

Robert seemed to suddenly realize he was holding another man's woman in his arms. He let her go and moved an appropriate distance from her. "Is that what ye truly want?"

Emilie dropped her head, shaking it in disbelief. "You know it's not, but I must do as I am told. I have no choice." How could she go through with this when the man she truly wanted stood there in front of her looking as though she'd stabbed him in the heart?

Robert regained his composure. "What of Edna? Will she no' help ye?"

"She wishes to help, but I my fate has already been written. I must marry Matteo."

"I've no' seen ye like this before. Perhaps ye should wait until the death of yer father is no' so fresh in yer mind." He reached out a hand to touch her, but withdrew it almost immediately when she backed away.

"You were the one who said our situation was impossible. That there was nothing we could do and so we should not see each other again." Why was he saying these things to her now? Why did he wait until the plans had all been made and she'd given her word to the Queen Mother that she would no longer resist this marriage?

Robert was quiet for a moment, as if collecting his thoughts. "I've given it much thought. If Edna can help, why no' let her?"

"I'm afraid it's too late." Emilie's tears had dried and her face was now without emotion. It had to be, because if she gave in for even a brief second, she would fall into his arms once again and beg him to take her away to a place far from here.

The look of sadness and disappointment that Robert was shrouded in was hard for Emilie to see, but he had been right all along. This is what she must do.

"Goodbye, Robert." She left him, ignoring the sound of his voice as he called to her. The life she thought had once been possible had only been a dream.

CHAPTER

# NINE

Robert hurried through the palace in search of Angus. He searched anywhere he thought he might find him. He had to meet with Edna. If everything he'd been told was true, then he would need her help and he was not above begging for it. Emilie was all that mattered to him. He didn't know how they could make things work considering the situation, but he would do anything. He had to at least try.

He was about to give up when he spied Edna and Angus leaving the palace together and ran to catch them.

"Angus, please stop," he shouted. "I must speak with ye and yer wife." This may be a fool's errand, but what choice did he have.

"Of course." Edna asked, reaching out a hand and placing it on his arm.

"It's Emilie. She says she's going to marry Barbieri as soon as it can be arranged." He'd accepted it when he thought they could not be together, but Angus had gotten his hopes up only to have them dashed when he spoke with Emilie in the garden. She was truly slipping away from him and the anguish he was feeling could not be disguised.

"Aye. She's said as much to us. The death of her father has her behaving in a way that I wasnae expecting." Edna shook her head as she spoke.

"Ye must help us. She told me about ye and the moon." The words sounded strange as they left his lips, he only hoped that it was all true and that Edna wouldn't think him daft.

As Edna gazed at him, Robert could feel her empathy and kindness and he relaxed. Everything would be fine. He could feel it.

"I can only do so much. If she doesnae want me help, it will be difficult to do what must be done."

"I understand that it will no' be easy, but I willnae give up. There has to be a way."

"I'm happy to hear ye say it, but there are nae guarantees. Now, we were just going to visit a friend," Edna said. "Would ye care to join us?"

"I would. Where are we going?" There was still hope. There had to be.

"To visit the woman who first gave Emilie the belief that ye could be together."

A FEELING of imminent danger surrounding Madame DuBois was the reason for today's journey to visit with her. Edna needed to be sure she was well and to be sure nothing was amiss. Her gut feelings were never wrong, so she was worried. They walked the short distance to Madame DuBois' abode. Once there, Edna knocked on her door only to find she wasn't home.

"Where could she be?" Angus asked.

"I doona ken, but I've had an uneasy feeling in the pit of me belly since we returned," Edna replied.

Robert peeked in the window. "She's no' there and her things seem to have been tossed about."

"We should go in," Edna said, pushing the door open. It was

shocking to see that all of the jars that had once been neatly placed on shelves around the room were now broken and strewn about the floor.

"I wonder what happened," Angus said.

"She's been accused of witchcraft. Two men came early this morning and took her away."

Edna spun around to find a man standing in the doorway. "Who are ye?"

"A neighbor and friend. I didn't dare try to stop them for fear they'd take me as well." The man wore a worried look on this face. His hat spun in his hands as he glanced around the room seeming nervous to be there.

"Do ye ken why she was taken?" Edna asked.

"She had a row with her neighbor yesterday. The woman in the cottage next door accused Madame DuBois of being a witch. I'm sure she contacted the authorities."

Edna's heart sank, "What were they fighting about? Do ye ken?"

"Everyone around here knew about it. It was a loud argument about Madame DuBois feeding stray cats. The neighbor woman is not fond of cats and it seems they had been sunning themselves all around her house. Madame Dubois and her neighbor had argued about it many times in the past, but Madame DuBois would not stop feeding them. She has a kind heart and would not see them starve."

Edna studied the neighbor carefully, wondering if she should ask the question on her mind, the one that could free Madame DuBois or seal her fate. Finally, she knew she had to ask. "Do ye believe she is a witch?" Edna asked carefully.

The neighbor barked out a laugh. "Not at all. She is just an old woman who loves animals. She grows herbs and vegetables in her garden and shares them with those in need."

"Thank ye." Edna was shocked and very worried. In this time being accused of witchcraft was a death sentence. "Angus, we must help her."

"Do ye ken where they've taken her?" Angus asked.

"She will be jailed at the Bastille while she awaits judgment," the man said. "It's not right. Can you help her?"

"I'm no' sure. This is no' good," Edna muttered to herself.

"We should go," Robert said, leading them back outside.

Once there were down the street, Angus asked, "Is there anything we can do?"

"I can speak with Louis. He may be able to intervene." Robert began walking away from the now empty home.

"Let's hope so." Edna's brain was whirling with thoughts. This was the very thing the woman had been afraid of. She had to help Madame DuBois after promising to protect her.

"Why did ye wish to see her?" Robert asked.

"I had a feeling that things were no' well here. My main thought was to check on Madame DuBois, but I also thought I would get some herbs that may help to ease Emilie's grieving. She is acting so irrationally. I must speak with her again. I must let her ken that her fate was no' predetermined by what her father wanted for her."

"She needs time to grieve, but instead is running away from her grief." Robert seemed perplexed by this behavior.

"We'll need to help her." Edna would do her best to help Emilie, but her focus was now on Madame DuBois, whose life was literally in grave danger.

ONCE BACK AT THE PALACE, Robert hurried off to the stables where he hoped to find Louis.

"Robert. I've been looking for you," Louis said, from atop his steed. "Where have you been?"

Robert stood beside Louis' horse, his hand gently stroking the steed's neck. "I was on an errand with a friend."

Louis seemed in good spirits. "I've had your horse prepared. Come ride with me."

The liveryman handed Robert the reins to his perfectly groomed and saddled gelding. That Louis was happy would make Robert's request all that much easier. He vaulted into the saddle and joined Louis who was warming his horse up by riding the outer edges of the arena. Once beside him he noted that Louis had that mischievous glint in his eye that usually meant trouble.

"I spied you earlier with your lady love here by the stables," Louis said, his voice a teasing lilt.

Robert couldn't deny it. "Emilie was telling me that her father had died and she began to cry. I only wished to comfort her."

"She hurried away. I imagine it did not work."

"Nae. It dinna."

"I'm sorry. It is difficult to lose one's father." There was a sadness in his tone that could not be denied. Louis had lost his own father and in his own way he wanted Robert to know that he understood and sympathized. "She didn't wish you to comfort her?"

"She doesnae ken what she wants. She's confused."

"It will take time. Do not give up hope." Louis could be difficult and childish, but in this moment he was giving Robert exactly what he needed, kindness and compassion.

They rode in silence for a while as Robert thought about Emilie and about the reason he'd sought out Louis in the first place. He wasn't sure how to bring up the topic of Madame DuBois. Should he just come right out with it? "Louis, I need yer help with something."

"Something to do with Emilie?" This seemed to pique Louis' interest.

"Nae. I doona think there is anything ye can do to help with Emilie. There is a woman here in Paris." Robert began his explanation and paused, unsure how to explain about the witch that wasn't a witch and needed to be released.

"Another? You are a busy man, Robert." Louis chuckled, back to his usual demeanor.

Keeping young Louis focused could be difficult. "I am being serious, Louis."

Louis raised an eyebrow at his friend. "Continue, please."

"She was arrested this morning. She is being accused of witchcraft."

Robert had Louis' attention now. "If she is a witch, I do not know what I can do to help."

"She is no' a witch." Robert knew that he was lying, but it was all he could think to do. "Her neighbor contacted the authorities. There was an argument about stray cats. The neighbor just wants her gone because of the cats." He glanced at Louis to see if he was truly listening.

"The poor are not above turning on each other," Louis said.

Robert knew the rich were just as likely to do the same but this didn't seem to be the time to mention it.

"So this is all about cats?" Louis was a bit suspicious about the direction this conversation had gone and Robert could certainly understand why. He had never asked the king for help with Emilie, the woman he loved, and yet here he was asking for the king to save a woman he didn't know.

"Is there anything ye can do to help her?" Robert prayed there was.

"Why is this so important to you?" Louis wondered.

"I doona wish to see someone punished for something as simple as feeding stray cats. Ye must admit that seems a poor reason for someone to face death." He waited, holding his breath for an answer.

"You are sure she is not a witch?" Louis slid his eyes to the side to look at Robert.

"She is no'. She is merely an old woman with an herb garden."

The king studied him for a moment longer, then seemed resolved. "I will help her. What is her name?"

"Madame DuBois."

As they approached the riding ring, Louis called to his footman who was always close at hand. "My quill and paper."

The man hurried away and Louis took his horse to a trot. Robert followed along beside him and they proceeded to take their horses through their daily paces. A short while later the man reappeared, holding the requested items out for Louis to take. Louis refused them. "I must dismount."

The man had his hands full with paper, quill and ink. On seeing this, Robert hopped down from his horse and held Louis' horse while he dismounted and then took the pen and paper. Louis went to a flat spot on the rail with his footman right behind him. He dipped the quill in the proffered ink and then scribbled away on the paper. When he was done, he handed a folded paper to the footman. "See that this is delivered immediately."

The man accepted the paper and bowing to Louis, turned and ran off to fulfill the task he'd been given.

"Thank ye, Louis. It is greatly appreciated." Robert was relieved for Madame DuBois.

Louis said nothing as he mounted his horse, setting off once again as though nothing had happened. They rode for a while longer, their conversation turned to lighter topics, which Robert noticed seemed to please Louis. The young king could be temperamental and difficult. It was good fortune that his mood had been light and nothing happened to change that before he'd written the note.

CHEWING ON HER LOWER LIP, Edna worried that they would be too late to help Madame DuBois. Hours had gone by since she'd last seen Robert and she was just about to go back to the inn when he appeared. She brightened considerably as he hurried her way. "Well?"

"Louis has taken care of it. She will be released." He beamed proudly as he spoke. "I would have come to tell ye sooner, but Louis was keeping me busy."

Edna sighed with relief. "I am grateful. Madame DuBois has been worried that someone would report her and thought that helping Emilie would be the cause of it."

"Do ye think that is the case?" Robert asked.

"Emilie knew it would be dangerous if she were to say anything to anyone at all," Edna said. "Nae. It was the neighbor. I am sure of it."

"Do ye wish to go to her?" Robert asked.

"Aye. I must be sure she is unharmed. I'll have to wait for Angus to return. He's gone off to find Matteo."

"There's nae need to wait for Angus. I'll go with ye. Ye'll need protection. As Louis' man nae one will question or bother ye."

"Thank ye, Robert. I can see why Emilie loves ye so." He was a kind and caring young man. He reminded her of Angus when he was that age. It made her nostalgic for those times when they were both young and in love. They'd been together many years now and their love had only grown deeper and more important. She wished the same for Robert and Emilie.

"I'll get a carriage to take us," Robert offered.

"That willnae be necessary. I'd like to walk." Her nerves had been jangling all day. A walk would give her time to clear herself of all the anxiety she'd been feeling, and it would also give her some time to get to know Robert a little better.

Robert extended his arm for her to take. Edna smiled up at him as they began to walk.

"Tell me about yerself, Robert. Why are ye here in Paris instead of back home in Scotland?"

"I came to Paris because I hoped there was more opportunity for me here."

Edna admired his initiative in creating his own path. "I can see ye were right. Look where ye've ended up. What do yer parents think of ye being so far from home?"

Robert expertly guided Edna out of the path of a wagon filled with vegetables headed to market. "Me parents are dead and me brothers were so busy fighting with each other over our land that nae one noticed I'd decided to leave." His tone was light and he seemed unbothered by what he was telling her.

"What a shame. I'm sure ye would have been a big help to them."

"Me brothers dinna believe so. I was the youngest and in their minds incapable of participating in matters involving the family lands. So I left."

Edna was curious about Robert's relationship with Louis. "And ye are now a guard to Louis XIII. How did that come about?"

"We met one day while I was riding along the river path. He was doing the same and was impressed with me horsemanship. He asked me to join him at the palace the next day with me horse. He is the king, which he reminds me often, and I am a soldier, but we have become friends."

"And so when ye asked him to free Madame DuBois, he agreed. He did it for ye."

Robert shrugged his shoulders. "He wouldnae care about a poor woman accused of witchcraft."

Edna turned their conversation to the reason she was in Paris. "How did ye meet Emilie?"

"At the palace. When I saw her, I immediately knew she was going to be me wife. I cannae believe I thought it was possible. We met in secret many times and I was pleased that she was exactly the woman I thought she would be when I first saw her. How could I no' love her?"

Edna heard the sadness in his voice and hoped she could fix things. "Doona lose faith. I've yet to fail in me attempts at bringing couples together."

Robert smiled. "I believe ye. I doona ken why, but I do."

"Ye'll find out why soon enough, lad," Edna chuckled.

They'd reached Madame DuBois' cottage and could hear the banging and clanging of things being tossed around inside. Robert held his hand out in front of Edna causing her to stop. He peeked in the doorway and a glass bottle was lobbed his way.

"Luckily she has poor aim," he said.

"Madame DuBois, 'tis Edna Campbell." She called through the door. "Please allow us to help ye."

"How did this happen? Who did this?" Madame DuBois seemed understandably distraught.

"There's nae way to ken," Edna said. "It could have been the authorities or yer neighbor."

"My neighbor has not been happy with me. She doesn't trust me and from the start thought I'd bring trouble. When it was cats that I brought, it was too much for her to take."

A small crowd gathered outside. None of the onlookers seemed happy to see Madame DuBois.

"Don't you worry. I will be leaving. I cannot stay here," she called to them.

"Good," someone from the small crowd shouted.

"Shall we go inside?" Edna asked.

Madame DuBois moved from the doorway, allowing them entrance.

"Are ye really planning to leave?" Edna asked.

"I have no choice." Madame DuBois looked around the mess that had been made and deflated a bit. "I cannot continue to live among these people. They now believe me to be a witch." She pointed towards the door. "They will come for me again. And next time I might deserve it."

"Ye've been so good to them. I was told ye shared yer vegetables and herbs with them."

"I did, but their minds have been poisoned by that one." She pointed in the direction of her neighbor's small hovel.

"Where will ye go?" Edna asked, her heart aching for the woman.

"Out to the countryside where no one will bother me." She continued sorting through the broken glass and not seeing anything salvageable, threw her hands in the air. "I've friends there so I won't be alone."

"I'm sorry it's come to this," Edna said. "I was hoping to get some herbs from ye."

"Look around," Madame DuBois said with disgust. "My herb

garden has been picked clean. They've destroyed everything. I've nothing left."

"Can we help ye pack what ye'll take with ye?" Robert asked.

Madame DuBois shook her head. "My bags are packed, and there's nothing here to salvage. I'm ready to be off." She picked up two fabric bags and slinging one over her shoulder and carrying one in her hand, she headed for the door.

"Good luck to ye," Edna called as she left them.

"What now?" Robert asked, once she was out of sight.

Edna looked around the room. Every single bottle had been broken. There were piles of loose powder everywhere and small puddles of liquid seeping into the dirt floor. It seemed that even the herbs had been stomped into oblivion. Whether it was the neighbors or the authorities, they'd done a thorough job of making anything they found as useless as possible. She continued searching, but finding nothing useful, turned to leave. "There's naething I can see that would be helpful."

Robert took her hand and guided her back out the door, being careful to avoid any broken glass. Once outside, he closed the door behind them and offered Edna his arm once again.

"I doona want ye to worry, Robert. I will make everything right for ye and Emilie." She sounded more sure of herself than she actually felt.

"I believe ye'll try," Robert said. It seemed he was being more realistic about her chances than she was.

The walk back to the palace gave Edna plenty of time to think, but other than kidnapping Emilie and taking her and Robert to the future, her mind was blank.

All she would have to do was fool them into joining her and Angus on a bridge, any bridge, and the rest would be easy. In the past she did not always have the permission of those she moved through time but the council let it be known she could no longer employ the methods of the past. To do so may ruin her chances of continuing on in her position. So now she found herself a witch who was somewhat powerless to resolve this situation with witchcraft.

When she'd started out on this journey two people needed her help and now one of them was making a different choice. It had been made clear to her by the council that she was only to help those who sought her help and so for now, she would continue to try to find another way to get through to Emilie. She was more determined than ever now that she'd gotten to know Robert and understood how much he loved Emilie.

# CHAPTER

# TEN

The beauty of the morning was lost on Edna as she joined Angus for breakfast. She had no appetite to speak of, but she'd sit with him while he ate. "I doona ken how to fix this." She'd tossed and turned all night long trying to come up with a solution and somehow Angus had managed to sleep through it all.

"Ye'll think of something. Ye always have," he assured her as he buttered a thick slice of bread and then topped it with jam.

"Maybe me luck has run out. Maybe it's time for me to fail." All these years of helping couples whether they wanted it or not had given her a sense of purpose and a great deal of satisfaction at the results. It troubled her that this may be the one time that love wouldn't win and there was nothing she could do about it.

Angus looked at her over the rim of his tea cup. "Now, the Edna I ken would never give up."

He was right. Edna was a fighter and she always fought for the things she believed in. She believed in love and it should be enough for her to win this battle. Edna sighed, resting her head in her hands before looking up at Angus once again.

"It was bad enough when all I had to do was overcome the fact that the Queen Mother had chosen a husband for Emilie and her father had agreed. Now Emilie has given up. She doesnae want to fight it anymore. What can I do about that?"

"Talk to her. She'll listen to ye." Angus was the calm voice of reason she needed to hear in that moment. He always had been.

"Something has to happen to change her mind. And then to change Matteo's mind." She tapped her fingers on the table as she thought.

Angus set his cup down on the table. "I'll talk to Matteo again. He's a bit on the miserly side, ye ken. He's told me he doesnae really want a wife. He wants his money all to himself. The only reason he's agreed to this marriage is the dowry he is to receive."

"That's it!" Edna practically jumped out of her chair. "The dowry. He willnae want to marry her if she has none."

Angus put his finger to his lips. Edna recognized this as him urging her to quiet down before everyone around them knew what they were discussing.

"How do ye ken her father dinna already pay the dowry?" Angus asked.

"From the looks of their family home, I cannae imagine he would have any money at all to offer." The tattered, peeling walls and the general disrepair hadn't happened overnight. That along with the fact that he'd only retained one servant were all good indications in Edna's mind.

"And yet, Matteo thinks he is getting a nice sum." Angus wrinkled his forehead with a frown.

"We'll have to find out. Do ye think Emilie would ken?" Edna's hopes were up once again. She could feel the thrill of imminent victory rushing through her body.

Angus shrugged his shoulders. "Ye'll have to speak with her, but she seemed surprised to find that they had nae money. I'm no' sure she kens any more than we do."

Edna thought about it for a moment. "That's probably true. Willnae Matteo and the Queen Mother be shocked when they find out." Feeling more sure of things, Edna's appetite reappeared as she nabbed some cheese from Angus' plate.

"Would ye like to get a plate of yer own?" Angus asked.

"I think I would." She grinned as she snuck another small bite of cheese.

"Good." Angus signaled to the man who'd brought his plate, letting him know Edna wanted to eat.

Before long a plate of bread, meats and cheeses was placed in front of her. "Thank ye," Edna said.

"You are most welcome, Madame."

She waited for the man to be out of ear shot before speaking again. "I feel better now. I think we've got a solution to our problem. When we're done here, we should head straight to the palace, doona ye think?"

"I think that if that is what ye want to do, then that's what we'll do," Angus said.

"Yer most agreeable this morning, Angus love." Edna hoped the love she was feeling for him was as evident to him as it was to her.

"Am I no' always agreeable?" he asked, with feigned affront.

"Ye are and I love ye for it." She blew him a kiss across the table.

Angus chuckled. "Finish yer breakfast now so we can be on our way."

Arriving at Tuileries, they were greeted by a servant with a note for Angus.

"Who's it from?" Edna asked, trying to take a peek at the note.

"Matteo." Angus looked over the piece of paper he held in his hand. "He'd like me to join him. He has something he wishes to discuss with me." He folded the paper and placed it in his sporran.

"Ye should go. I'll see if I can find Emilie." If all went well, Edna thought they might be able to solve this dilemma today.

Angus headed off with the servant and Edna made her way to the throne room where she hoped to find Emilie.

Several women were present, all ladies-in-waiting to Marie de Medici. Edna marveled at their gowns. They were each beautiful in their own way. Satins and silks with ribbons and embroidery that depicted flowers, trees, birds and deer. Edna knew from her own experience with seventeenth century dress that it took forever to don an outfit, especially without help. The clothing of the time was made for beauty, not comfort.

Edna smiled in greeting as she entered the room. Each footstep echoed loudly as she walked. The high ceilings and vast expanse of the room would be ideal for eavesdropping. Of course, when it was crowded with people it was not a concern, but this morning with only the ladies-of-the-court present, every word they uttered carried easily from one end of the room to the other.

Her goal had been to find Emilie so they could chat, but she wasn't present. Edna was about to leave when the Queen Mother arrived and walked straight towards her.

"Madame Campbell, how are you this morning?" Marie asked.

Edna curtsied deeply to the Queen Mother. "I am well, Yer Highness. I was looking for Emilie."

"She is being fitted for the dress she is to be wed in," Marie said.

"I see. When is the wedding to take place?" This was information Edna desperately needed.

"Tomorrow at the chapel here at Tuileries." Marie looked past Edna at someone entering the room and apparently finding them less than interesting turned back to Edna.

"So soon?" Edna asked, feeling a surge of panic hitting her once again.

Marie chuckled. "It seems our bride is in a hurry to marry."

"I was hoping to speak with her this morning," Edna said.

"She is in the room at the top of the stairs with the dressmaker. I'm sure she would value your opinion of her dress. Why don't you join her?"

"I think I will." Edna curtsied to the Queen Mother once again and hurried from the room.

At the top of the stairs, she entered a small room where Emilie stood on a round riser while the dressmaker marked the hem for her dress. It was a pretty, pale blue satin fabric, as a show of Emilie's purity. Long panels of ecru lace ran the length of the gown from bodice to hem, leaving the center fabric to shine on its own. The sleeves were puffed to the elbows and then cinched there with embroidered ribbon before continuing in a more slender form to the wrist. The hem of the sleeves was decorated with the same lace used to create the fan-shaped reticella that rose from the neckline of the dress to stand up behind her head. She looked like a princess in every respect except one. She seemed terribly unhappy.

"Emilie," Edna said. "Ye look beautiful."

Emilie lifted her downturned eyes to gaze at Edna. "Thank you, but I do not feel beautiful."

"I willnae argue with ye, but I see a beautiful young woman ready to start a new life." Edna's voice lacked the enthusiasm one might expect at a moment like this. Emilie's beauty in this moment should be shared with Robert, not Matteo.

"Would you excuse us for a few moments?" Emilie said to the woman marking the dress.

"Of course. I'll be right outside when you're ready to continue." She left the room, closing the door behind her.

"Emilie, we must talk." Edna walked closer and could see dark circles under the young woman's eyes. "I have an important question for ye."

Emilie stepped down from the riser she'd been standing on.

Edna took Emilie's hands in hers. "I ken we discovered that yer father was destitute before his death. I wonder, did he arrange a dowry for ye?"

A wide-eyed gaze met Edna's question. "I don't know," Emilie stammered. "He didn't discuss those matters with me. Perhaps the

Queen Mother knows." Emilie ran her hands down the front of her dress, but there didn't appear to be any pleasure there.

"If he dinna, doona be surprised if Matteo doesnae wish to marry ye." Edna was bubbling with excitement, which she did her best to contain while she waited for Emilie's reaction.

Her face a mass of confusion, Emilie took a moment before speaking. A tiny hint of hope appeared. "What do you mean?"

"This could be exactly what we'd hoped for. If Matteo willnae marry ye, then ye'd be free to be with Robert." Edna could see her excitement wasn't moving Emilie in the way she'd expected it would. The elation she'd expected simply wasn't there.

"I'm sure my father would have seen to it that everything was in place when they made the agreement." There was an uncertain tone in her voice as though she was unsure about pinning her hopes on what might only be a pipe dream.

Her reply was a bit defensive, and while it made sense that she was protecting her father's name, Edna still couldn't tell whether Emilie was happy about this possibility or not. "Do ye agree that it would be a good thing?"

"I am to be married tomorrow. I don't see how that will change," Emilie said. Emotion seemed to have been drained from her as there was none in her voice or her face as she spoke.

"I do." Edna was adamant. "I must figure out how this all works. Is there a marriage agreement? Has it been fulfilled? What would happen if it is no'?"

Emilie's response was sharp and unexpected. "I do not know the answers to any of those questions. I will not get my hopes up only to have them dashed once again. Now, if you'll excuse me I'd like to finish with my dress."

Edna couldn't understand why Emilie was behaving like this. She should be happy that there may be an opportunity to get out of this marriage, but instead she seemed irritated that Edna would even mention it to her. Dismissed as she had been, Edna left the room and hoped that there would be some way to get the information she needed.

ANGUS KNOCKED on the door of Matteo's room and was greeted by a servant. The decor of the room was simple in comparison to every other room Angus had seen at Tuileries, but more than comfortable by his standards. Matteo was seated in a cushioned chair reading when Angus arrived.

"Angus, I am happy you are here." Matteo stood and greeted Angus at the door.

"What can I do for ye, Matteo?" Angus asked, wondering why on earth Matteo needed to see him.

"I wonder if you would be present when I meet with the Queen Mother." Matteo raised his eyebrows in question as he waited for Angus to answer.

"Of course, I'd be happy to join ye. What is this meeting about?" Angus didn't have a clue as to what Matteo was about to tell him.

"No mention has been made about Emilie's dowry. Her father is now deceased and I am not sure where the dowry is." Matteo's face was a mixture of worry, frustration and irritation.

"Ye mean ye havenae received it yet?" Angus asked.

"I would not expect to receive it until after we are married, but no plans were made for the transfer of the dowry to my name. I am hoping the Queen Mother will have the answers."

Angus was wondering the very same thing and voiced his opinion. He hoped he wasn't overstepping his bounds here, but felt it was unfair for Matteo to be left in the dark. "Matteo, I have been concerned about the verra same thing. When Edna and I joined Emilie at her father's estate, we were shocked to see it in terrible disrepair and with only one servant present to care for the man."

"Do you think there is no dowry?" Matteo's voice rose in pitch as that thought seemed to make its way into his brain.

"I doona ken. I would have thought that was already taken care of." This was turning out to be an interesting turn of events. Matteo didn't know where the dowry was. Marie hadn't said anything about it. Angus was fairly sure there was no dowry and if he was right, things were about to take a turn.

"I must find out. If there is no dowry, there will be no wedding," Matteo slammed his fist into his palm.

That was fine with Angus. He liked Matteo and knew how he felt about marrying, so if it was the case that Emilie had no dowry, everyone would be happy. Or so he hoped.

"When is this meeting?" Angus asked.

"Tomorrow morning." Matteo's attention seemed to be fluctuating between Angus and his own thoughts.

"Arenae ye getting married tomorrow?" Angus cocked a brow in query.

"Yes, but not until late afternoon. The Queen Mother has everything planned." Matteo began pacing back and forth in front of Angus.

"She willnae be happy if it's no' going to work out," Angus said.

"I cannot help that." His voice was filled with indignation. "If I've been lied to, then I have every right to decline the marriage."

"I'll be here bright and early tomorrow for the meeting then," Angus assured him.

"Thank you, my friend. I have been blessed to meet you here in this place where I feel very much the stranger."

Angus was touched by Matteo's words. He had grown fond of him since their first meeting. He was a knowledgeable man, who spoke with authority on many subjects. He had mentioned to Angus more than once that he felt out of place here at Tuileries and that he would be happy when it was time to go back to his home.

Angus knew how he felt. While he was enjoying his time here in the court of Louis XIII, he couldn't wait to get back home to his big comfy chair, cozy fire and his newspapers. He was very much a creature of habit and wondered what he might have missed out on while he was here in France.

"I wonder if ye'd like to join me for a walk. I find I need some fresh air on this beautiful day." Angus understood Matteo must be feeling nervous about tomorrow and he wished to be as supportive as possible. After all, he may soon be responsible for a wife.

"I would like that very much," Matteo said, patting Angus on the back.

They walked along the banks of the Seine, enjoying the sights and sounds of the river and its flora and fauna.

"Matteo, I ken the idea of a wife is no' one ye've had before this, but what of children? Would ye like to have a son to carry on yer bloodline?"

"I have barely accepted that I will have a wife. I am not interested in children."

Angus thought his words interesting. "No' even to have an heir?"

Matteo stopped and faced the water, scanning the surface as an otter playfully appeared and disappeared. "My will has been prepared. When I die, my money will go to the church as I've always intended."

"What about Emilie?" Angus wondered. If they went through with this marriage she would be left alone in a foreign country.

"She will receive a small stipend that should last her the rest of her days. If she marries, the money would then go to the church." The otter appeared again, bringing a small smile to his face.

"Ye've really given this a lot of thought," Angus said.

"Of course. I do not wish my money wasted on frivolities and so it was important to me to have a plan."

Angus had to admire Matteo's attention to his financial details even if he didn't agree with him. He and Edna weren't rich, but they'd always had enough. There were so many more things in life that were important. Things that money couldn't buy, love and happiness among them. He wondered if Matteo had ever been in love and asked him.

"Once, a very long time ago," Matteo said.

"What happened, if ye doona mind me asking?"

"It is too complicated to explain. Our love was not meant to be." A bit of melancholy sounded in his voice.

"And ye've never been in love since?" Angus was surprised by this.

"Never. I would not allow myself such a luxury. It is too painful when things end."

Angus might have said that love doesn't have to end, but he realized there was more here than he was being told and left it at that. He felt sad for Matteo. Sad that he'd never had someone in his life the way that Angus had Edna. Someone who would be there no matter what life presented. Sad that he looked on marriage as a financial burden and children as another drain on his wealth. Angus and Edna considered themselves lucky to have their daughter. She had chosen to live in another century and they missed her terribly, but there were others in their lives who helped to fill the void left by her absence. He thought about Maggie and Dylan and hoped that they were well and that they'd wait for them to return home before those wee twins were born. He placed a hand on Matteo's shoulder.

"Yer a good man, Matteo. I wish ye naething but happiness from this day forth."

"I wish the same for you, my friend." A sad smile came and went quickly from his face. "Perhaps you will visit me in Rome sometime."

Matteo had mentioned this once before and Angus found no harm in offering some hope. "If it is possible, I will be happy to come for a visit."

They continued their walk, marveling at the brilliant white swans floating nearby, the kestrels, cormorants and more otters were spotted bobbing in the rippling waters of the Seine. Angus was happy he'd made a new friend, but sad he'd probably never see him again once he went back home.

CHAPTER

# ELEVEN

Edna closed the door to their room at the inn and let out a deep sigh. Things weren't going the way she had hoped. Angus started a fire in the hearth and Edna stared at it as a thought came to mind. "I'm going to contact Maggie. Maybe she can help me sort this all out."

Sitting comfortably in front of the fire, Edna stared into the flames and reached out to her niece. "Maggie, are ye there?" Edna waited a few moments before asking again. "Maggie, it's me, yer Auntie Edna. I need yer help. Are ye there?"

The flames flared and parted as Maggie appeared. "I'm here, Auntie. Where are ye?"

"I'm in France. Paris to be exact, at the court of Louis XIII at Tuileries Palace."

"Wow! Sounds like fun," Maggie said, shifting around in her chair.

"Ye look uncomfortable, dear. Is everything going to plan with the pregnancy?"

"All is well, but aye, uncomfortable. Poor Dylan is having to do everything around here. It's gotten just so hard to do even the simplest of chores. I cannae even see me toes!"

Edna chuckled. She needed this. Her stress level had been through the roof over the past few days, "Have ye shut down the inn yet?"

"The last guests left this morning. We'll stay closed until after the babies arrive."

"Promise me ye'll wait for us to return. We'll head straight there after we get back." Edna couldn't wait to meet the new bairns and she was worried that her mission here was taking much longer than anticipated.

"I'm no' sure I can make that promise. It depends on when ye'll be back."

"I'm hoping it willnae be much longer. I'm having a difficult time with the young lass who called me here."

Maggie yawned. "Sorry. I havenae been sleeping well. These little ones are up all night. Seems like they're having a wrestling match in there."

"I wish I was there with ye," Edna said. "I could help with so many things."

"We've got it all under control," Maggie assured her. "Ye've got enough to worry about where ye are. So, tell me why this lass is giving ye trouble."

"She is determined to go through with a marriage that neither she nor the groom want," Edna's exasperation was evident in her voice.

"If neither wants it, what's the problem?" Maggie asked.

"Her father has passed away and she feels she is honoring his last wishes. The wedding is tomorrow." She shook her head in disbelief.

"Then ye doona have much time to sort this out." Maggie paused for a moment, closing her eyes. "I'm getting the feeling there is someone else involved. I'm sensing some deceit around the groom."

"Ye think the groom is being deceitful?" Edna asked. She thought about Matteo and how forthcoming he had been with his feelings about marriage, she hadn't thought him even capable of deceit.

Maggie shook her head. "No' the groom. Someone else."

"I think you are on to something with that, Maggie me love."

"I think if ye can find that person, yer troubles with the bride will be settled."

"Oh, Maggie, darlin', I do miss ye so. I'd better have success with this couple or I may be back to living in Glendaloch."

"Ye ken we'd love that." Maggie smiled warmly and blew her a kiss.

"I ken and if that's what happens, so be it." She would accept the decision of the council, but in her heart, she wanted to get this right. Emilie and Robert belonged together, she knew that. There was so much at stake here. "It's just that Angus and I had plans for so many adventures together before we retire."

"Auntie, I think I'm losing me connection here. I can't wait to see ye and Uncle! I love ye both."

"Goodbye, dear. We'll see ye soon."

Maggie's face faded into the fire. Edna reluctantly stood and walked to the window. Angus joined her, standing at her shoulder as she looked out on the small courtyard below.

"Did yer chat with Maggie help?" Angus asked.

"Ye heard what she said. Someone is being deceitful."

"If I had to guess, there are only two people it could be. Marie or Concini."

"Me thoughts exactly. What would they have to gain though? Arranging a marriage for a girl with nae dowry is kind-hearted, but I doona think either of those two would be doing this out of the kindness of their hearts." She glanced out to the street. It was dark and quiet. "Emilie kens naething at all about the dowry. It's apparent nae one has said anything to her."

Angus rubbed Edna's shoulders as he spoke. "Matteo's in the dark as well. He hasnae heard anything at all. He asked me to join him in the morning to speak with Marie about it."

"That should be an interesting meeting, doona ye think?"

"I'm sure it will be. He has already told me that if there is nae dowry there will be nae wedding."

"That's a good thing. I guess we should pray there is none. Although Emilie is still behaving verra strangely. It's as though she is marrying Matteo out of a sense of duty nae matter what happens. I got the impression that if there was nae dowry it would be a disappointment to her."

"She is only interested is fulfilling her father's wishes. I can understand that, especially since it was his last wish."

"Ye're right. The poor lass has been through so much of late. It's nae wonder she feels her world has gone all topsy-turvy." She had sympathy for Emilie. She really did, but Edna wasn't about to let Emilie's doubts derail her. "She called us here with her heartfelt wish on the moon and now she's behaving like the idea that I want to see her and Robert together is a ridiculous one. My job is to fix things, but I need a little cooperation from Emilie."

"It will all come to a head soon enough." Angus once again remained cool and calm in the face of Edna's rising irritation.

"I can only do so much without spelling her and I really doona want to do that. I think the dowry thing will take care of half of the issue." She thumped her lower lip with her index finger as she thought.

Angus took her hand stopping her. "Listen to me. Maybe once she realizes Matteo willnae marry her, she'll come out of this grief-driven melancholy she's been in."

"I hope so. Otherwise, I'll be heading back to the Council of Witches as a failure, and on me first job." Edna let out a deep sigh as her shoulders slumped.

Angus tipped her chin up and looked into her eyes. "Edna, love, ye have never failed anyone in need of yer help. Ye willnae fail this time." He pulled Edna into his arms, wrapping her in a warm hug. "Ye worry too much."

"I ken I do, but it's so obvious that Robert and Emilie should be together. It would be unimaginable if things dinna work out for them."

"We'll ken soon enough." Angus kissed the tip of her nose and Edna nestled into his arms.

"That's what scares me. I was hoping to have more time, but now everything is moving full steam ahead."

"That it is, me love. That it is." He rested his chin atop her head.

"I'm mentally, physically and emotionally exhausted." She allowed Angus to guide her across the room.

"Come then. Let's get ye into bed. Would ye want some tea?" Angus asked as he helped her out of her dress.

"Nae thank ye. I just need some sleep. My head is going to need to be clear for tomorrow." Edna slipped a shift over her head and climbed into bed.

"Did ye see Robert today?" Angus asked, tucking her in.

"Nae. I dinna." Edna rested her weary head on her pillow, closing her eyes.

"Neither did I," Angus said, climbing into the bed beside her, blowing out the bedside candle.

"I wonder where he was."

"I thought I heard one of Louis' servants say something about hunting." He rolled to face Edna, placing a protective arm across her waist.

"If he's away it's probably for the best. He willnae want to be present if, despite our efforts, Emilie ends up marrying Matteo."

Louis XIII watched as his men set up the massive royal tent they'd brought along with them. Leaving the palace yesterday morning, they'd taken their time traveling to their final hunting spot. "This is an ideal time for a hunting trip, don't you agree, Robert?"

"What's different about today than any other day for hunting?"

Robert asked, not really caring what the answer might be as his thoughts were elsewhere.

"Nothing really." Louis said. "I was tiring of life at court. I was bored and my mother was being maddening. I had to get away from her."

Robert only nodded and listened. Louis and Marie were at odds more often than not and he'd heard all about it on many an occasion. Marie was having a difficult time adjusting to the fact that Louis had come of age faster than she liked and would soon be king.

Louis gave Robert a sideways glance before continuing. "All she can talk about is Emilie and Barbieri and the wedding."

Robert closed his eyes, exhaling his frustrations regarding Emilie.

"I'm sorry. I probably shouldn't talk about that with you, should I?" Louis asked.

Robert knew him well enough to know that he had purposely chosen this topic knowing it would be upsetting to him. "Ye are the king. Ye can speak of whatever ye wish."

"You know the wedding is tomorrow, or hadn't you heard?" Louis asked.

"Nae. I hadnae heard." Robert tried not to look shocked and did his best to calm the urge to hop on his horse and race back to the palace. He couldn't believe she was going through with it, although what choice did she really have? The thing that bothered him was how she changed course on him. One day she was convinced Edna would solve all their problems and then, after her father's death, she was convinced she was going to marry Barbieri because it had been her father's wish. There was nothing he could do about it, but in his heart he wanted to save her from herself.

"What are you thinking?" Louis asked.

Exasperated, his response to Louis was anything but the way one should respond to a king. "Why do ye care? Do ye wish to bait me even further with talk of Emilie and her marriage?"

"You sound frustrated," Louis observed, seeming unfazed by Robert's response to his question.

"I am frustrated. There is naething I can do to stop what is about to happen. I thought I'd have time to convince her..."

"To convince her of what?" Louis asked.

Robert tossed aside his irritation with Louis. "To convince her that she should be with me. That she should disobey everyone who has control over her and run away with me."

"You could still do that." Louis seemed to be having a moment of wisdom.

"How?" Robert asked.

"Ride back to the palace. Find her. Tell her your plan. If she loves you, she will defy my mother to be with you."

"Ye want me to do this because it would make yer mother angry. Am I correct?"

A crooked smirk appeared on Louis' face. "You are."

He didn't care what Louis' motivation was. What mattered to Robert was whether or not he could convince Emilie she was making a mistake she would regret for the rest of her life. He had to try. He couldn't forgive himself if he didn't. He gazed at Louis, who seemed beside himself with glee.

"Go!" Louis said.

"I doona think I should leave ye. What if ye need me?" For Robert, his duty to the king always came first and although he wanted nothing more than to leave, he had sworn an oath of duty to the king.

"Do you not see the many men here? If they cannot be of service then I have chosen the wrong group to accompany me."

Robert glanced around the field. There were several very capable guards and servants present. Louis was right. He'd be fine without Robert.

"I will see ye back at court," Robert said as he vaulted onto his horse and galloped away. Emilie would hear what he had to say and he would accept her answer, no matter what it was.

～

"Are ye ready, Matteo?" Angus greeted Matteo outside of the throne room.

"Angus, thank you for joining me. Shall we go in?"

"Matteo, I see you out there. Come in." Marie de Medici's voice carried to where they stood.

The men looked at each other with raised eyebrows then entered the room where Marie was seated and waiting for them. "Your Highness." Both men bowed to her.

"You will be married this afternoon." Marie gazed at Matteo with the confident air of a woman who made announcements that brooked no argument.

"Before we discuss the wedding, I must ask about Emilie's dowry. Now that her father has died, I have questions." It was clear Matteo would not be cowed by Marie.

"Questions. Whatever for?" Marie snapped back at him.

"The marriage was arranged between you and Comte Toussaint. I was not involved in the discussions. I was assured that there would be a substantial dowry, but I have not seen evidence of it."

"Comte Toussaint assured me there would be a dowry and that is all you need to know." She waved a dismissive hand at Matteo.

"If there is a dowry, where is it?" Matteo asked, sounding like a man that would not be put off by Her Royal Highness.

Marie was becoming irritated. "May I remind you that you are speaking to the Queen Mother?"

"My apologies, Your Highness. I did not mean to offend you. It's just that Angus here was with Emilie when her father died and noticed some peculiarities that you may be unaware of."

Marie gazed at Angus appearing quite displeased. "Well..."

"Yer Highness, me wife and I noticed that his home was in disrepair and that he had but one servant left to care for him. It seems he told Emilie that he had lost everything and that he'd only been allowed to stay in his home because he would die soon."

Marie's immediate response was suspicious. She silently glared at Angus as though she were thinking of what to say next. It seemed to Angus that she was aware of this all along.

"Why was I not made aware of this?" Marie asked, glancing around for someone to blame.

"I doona ken, Yer Highness," Angus said.

"Bertrand!" she shouted.

A bespectacled man rushed into the room. "Yes, Your Highness."

"Did Comte Toussaint make arrangements for Emilie Toussaint's dowry?"

"I have not seen anything to this point," Bertrand's voice shook as he spoke.

Marie eyed him angrily.

"I will go look through the records." He hurried from the room.

"No matter. Dowry or no dowry, you will marry this afternoon."

"Your Highness. The only reason I agreed to this marriage was because I would receive a handsome dowry. I'm afraid I cannot go through with it until I am assured I will be compensated."

Marie's eyes narrowed as she stared at Matteo. She was angry, that much was apparent. Again, it seemed to Angus that she was behaving suspiciously. In his mind, she knew more than she was letting on.

"Then the wedding will need to be postponed. It may take Bertrand some time to locate the documents we seek." She stood and marched out of the room, addressing her curtsying ladies on the way through the doors. "Find me Emilie Toussaint immediately."

"That went well," Angus chuckled.

"She is quite angry," Matteo replied. "Not as angry as I will be should there be no dowry. She will not force me into this marriage, I promise you."

"She seemed determined that the wedding would take place." At least that was the essence of what Angus had heard.

"Without money, the girl is no better than a pauper. I feel sorry for her, but I will not marry her."

EMILIE KNOCKED on the door of the Queen Mother's private rooms. She was nervous. The ladies-of-the-court had found her in the garden and told her the Queen Mother was angry and needed to see her.

"Come in," Marie called.

"You wished to see me, Your Highness." Emilie curtseyed and then held her hands in front of her to stop them from shaking. Marie did not seem angry now. Perhaps the ladies had been mistaken.

Marie examined Emilie from head-to-toe before speaking. "I understand that your father was impoverished at the time of his death. Do you understand this to be true?"

"I'm afraid so. I do not know how it happened." Emilie was surprised that the Queen Mother would be unaware of this. It is not something her father would want to be public knowledge, but surely he told the Queen Mother when they met to arrange the betrothal.

"What of your dowry?" Marie asked. She held her hand out in front of herself and examined her nails as she waited for Emilie to answer.

"I don't know anything about my dowry, Your Highness. I thought my father had arranged everything when he last visited the palace." This wasn't a topic that would have been discussed with her, and the Queen Mother knew that.

"I'm sorry to say that if we cannot find proof of a dowry, Matteo will not marry you."

She certainly didn't sound sorry, but her words did give Emilie some hope that she would not have to marry a man she didn't love. "I see." If the marriage did not take place, she wondered what would happen to her. Where would she go? Would Robert still want her after she'd pushed him away for what seemed the last time?

"We have postponed the wedding until we have our answers," Marie stated.

"What will happen if I have no dowry?" Emilie asked, not sure she wanted to hear the answer. Her stomach was in knots and her knees were so weak she thought she might faint.

"That is something I must decide. You will be too poor to stay here at court." She wandered to the window and gazed out onto the courtyard. "There is always the convent. Or I may be able to convince Barbieri that it is best that he marry you." She turned to Emilie. "There is no point in making decisions until we have word from Bertrand. Go. I will call you when I know."

Emilie left the room feeling several emotions all at one time. Excitement that she may not have to marry Matteo. Anxiety at not knowing what would become of her. Lastly, a small amount of hope built in her that she might be able to be with Robert.

Wandering outside to sit under her favorite chestnut tree, Emilie couldn't help but be nervous about her future. As she sat trying to clear her mind, she noticed a horse speeding through the garden to the stable. Could it be Robert? She stood to get a better look. It was Robert. His stature, build and kilt were unmistakable even at a distance. She watched as he dismounted and put his horse away before heading back toward the palace. She dared not call to him as it would draw unwanted attention, but she hurried in his direction, practically running as she lifted her skirts.

Robert must have heard her as she ran because he turned to see her coming. He ran to meet her, taking her by the arm and guiding her away from the palace to a secluded spot in the garden they'd found months ago, by a copse of trees on the edge of a pond.

Their secret spot was filled with the sounds of insects buzzing, birds chirping and the leaves of the trees rustling as squirrels playfully hopped from branch to branch above their heads. It was a beautiful spot, but one that Emilie had avoided of late. She didn't wish for her recent troubles to taint a spot that held such wonderful memories. Memories she'd made with Robert at a time before her betrothal.

"Robert I must speak to you," Emilie said, out of breath from rushing to meet him.

"And I ye," Robert answered.

"What is it?" Emilie asked, wanting to hear what he had to say before she bared her heart to him. The way he was looking at her made her heart beat a little faster. Her hand flew to her belly to quell the butterflies there.

"I cannae let ye go through with this Emilie. I love ye and I wish ye to be me wife." The earnestness of his words touched her heart.

"I wish that as well, Robert." Emilie was relieved. She hadn't chased him away for good as she'd thought. He still wanted her to be his wife.

"I ken ye are to marry Barbieri, but we could run away together. We could go back to Scotland. They wouldnae come searching for us there." He reached out to brush a strand of hair from her eyes.

"We may not need to go to such lengths. It may be that my father did not leave a dowry for me. Matteo does not wish to marry me without one. There will be no wedding today. The Queen Mother has decided we will wait until the papers from my father are found."

A brilliant smile reached Robert's eyes as he took her in his arms. "That is good news."

"I am poor, Robert. I have nothing. Do you still want me?" Emilie had no idea what it meant to be poor and it frightened her, but if she had Robert she could face anything life brought her way.

His answer didn't disappoint her. "More than I've ever wanted anything."

Robert dipped his head, taking her lips in a tender kiss. Emilie wrapped her arms around his neck, her fingers tangling in his thick, dark curls. "I love you, Robert MacMillan."

She felt Robert's hands as they massaged her back, and then moved to cup her breasts. His kisses streamed down her neck and along her collarbone. Shivers of delight ran down her spine as he held her close, their bodies touching from head to toe. Through the many layers of her gown she could feel the hardness of his desire for her.

Emilie placed her hands on his chest, pushing back a bit to see his face. "Robert, we must stop before we cannot."

He reluctantly loosened his hold and taking her head in his hands gave her one final kiss. A kiss that melted her heart and made her knees weak. "Soon." he said.

"Soon," she repeated.

Robert leaned back against one of the trees that had been shielding them from view. "I'm happy Louis sent me back from our hunting trip, although his reasons were more for his satisfaction than he thought they would be mine."

"How so?" Emilie asked, curious as to why Louis would want to help them.

"He enjoys getting under his mother's skin. He thought if I came to get ye it would anger her." Robert shook his head and chuckled.

"She doesn't have to know," Emilie said, her lips curving into a sweet smile.

"Do ye believe there really is nae dowry?" He asked. His voice was filled with hope.

"I'm not sure. All I know is that my father wanted me to marry Matteo so that I would be taken care of. It was his dying wish." Her voice cracked and suddenly her throat felt tight.

Robert took her in his arms once again. This time it was to comfort her. "He loved ye and wanted what was best for ye. I understand his concern. He was a good father to ye."

Emilie fought back the tears that threatened to open wounds that were still healing. He wiped a tear from her cheek and whispered, "All will be well. I am sure of it."

Emilie melted into his embrace. This is what she wanted more than anything – to love and be loved. Whatever the outcome, she was a woman who knew what she wanted. The question was, would she get it?

CHAPTER

# TWELVE

The following morning Edna and Angus returned to the palace hoping for news about Emilie's nuptials. The walk there took them along the path that had become quite familiar to them. It was a busy morning in Paris. They passed numerous people on their way. Some were heading to the palace as they were, some were heading towards the Seine to walk, others stood in small groups chatting happily with each other. Edna steered Angus towards the small bakery where she'd bought bread with Emilie the day they'd walked together. They purchased some brioche and candied chestnuts and ate them as they walked. All-in-all it seemed like the perfect morning. Edna had her fingers crossed that it would continue to be and that there was no dowry so then Matteo would refuse the marriage.

Once at the palace, they made their way through the courtyard where they came upon Robert, who seemed quite happy to see them.

"Good morn," Robert said. "'Tis a beautiful day do ye no' think?" He spread his arms out to indicate the clear blue skies above them.

"Yer in good spirits this morning, Robert," Angus said, slapping him on the back.

"I've good reason," Robert said. Wearing a wide grin that spread to his bright, happy eyes.

"What have ye heard?" Edna latched onto his arm, steering him away from those who might eavesdrop on their conversation.

"Naething yet, but there is every possibility that there is nae dowry." Edna loved seeing him this happy. Since their arrival in Paris, there had always been an air of solemnity about him that rarely changed.

Angus cleared his throat as he glanced at Edna and then back to Robert. "The only trouble is that yesterday, Marie seemed inclined to force Matteo to marry Emilie, dowry or nae dowry."

Robert scowled on hearing this. "She will run away with me if that is the case. We spoke yesterday."

"That is wonderful. I've been on pins and needles since we saw ye last. I hope we ken soon." Edna's mind was racing regardless of the hopeful news. Things could go either way and they needed to be prepared for that.

"Aye. I've made plans to meet her in the garden this morning. We will discuss our departure at that time."

"All is going well then. Ye hardly needed me," Edna said.

Robert glanced around for anyone who may be eavesdropping before he spoke. "We may need ye yet."

"How so?" Edna asked. She was determined to help in any way possible.

"We may need a diversion so we can be far from here before anyone thinks to look for us." Robert said. "Emilie wants to wait to hear about the dowry before we go."

"Whatever for? Why no' go now?" Edna asked. If she had her druthers, that would be her choice for them.

"She doesnae wish to run away unless it is necessary. The Queen Mother may decide to drag her back," Robert explained. "If there is nae dowry, the Queen Mother willnae want her here at court. She will nae longer concern herself with Emilie marrying a soldier. Why should she? The only problem would be if she decided Emilie must go through with the marriage."

"I see. So she believes Marie will send her on her way if she has nae money." Edna wished she could be as sure as Robert and Emilie. Marie was a hard one to read, and she had a reputation for making rash decisions.

"Aye. That is what we believe," Robert confirmed.

"Let's pray it's that easy." Edna tried to keep the worry from her voice, not wanting to put a damper on Robert's mood.

"I must go. Emilie will be waiting for me." He hurried off through the courtyard toward the garden.

"Off with ye then," Angus said. He turned to Edna once Robert was gone. "We may be on our way home sooner than we thought."

"I want to see Maggie and Dylan. The babies will be coming any day now." Edna always had her family in her thoughts and she'd been sure to let Maggie know exactly that when they'd spoken through the fire. Being there for Maggie when the twins came would be her number one priority once she and Angus were back home. "Maggie will need our help. We may need to stay for a week or two until they get into a routine with the bairns. I'd like to be there before they need us, if possible."

"As would I. It'll be nice to see the inn and all our old friends. I ken it hasnae been that long, but I do miss them." Angus wrapped an arm around Edna's shoulders, giving her a squeeze.

Edna responded with an arm around his waist. "It would be wonderful to see them and we can always invite them to visit us in Edinburgh, as well. We have a spare room for guests."

Angus turned to her and in all seriousness said, "Let's finish what we came to do then."

"We should find Matteo and see if he's heard anything yet."

Angus extended his elbow for Edna to take and they headed into the palace hoping for good news.

～

"Matteo," Angus called, seeing him waiting for Marie in the throne room. They headed his way, eager to hear any news.

The room was busier than usual that morning. It seemed many people required an audience with Marie. They stood around in small groups here and there. The hubbub of voices filled the room, allowing them to speak without fear of being overheard.

"Good morning, Angus." He bowed his head as they approached. "Madame Campbell."

"Good morn to ye," Edna said. "Any word?"

"Not yet. They are still searching for anything that Comte Toussaint may have sent to the palace before his death." He seemed more troubled this morning and Angus wondered if there was more than the dowry that was bothering him.

"They doona seem verra organized," Edna noted.

"Not at all." Matteo paced back and forth for a bit before stopping in front of Angus. "The Queen Mother has threatened me."

"Threatened ye? How?" Angus asked, as Edna drew closer.

"She has told me that even without a dowry I must marry Emilie. She says that Concini has information about me that would destroy my standing in Rome."

"Do ye ken what it is?" Angus asked.

"Possibly."

Angus hoped he'd say more, but it was Matteo's business and if he didn't wish to share it with him, Angus understood.

"Why is this so important to her? If Emilie has nae dowry then it should be a settled matter. It's odd that she would push for the marriage, doona ye agree?" Edna was baffled. "Why on earth would Marie even care?"

"She can be a spiteful woman. She is angry with me for some slight she accuses me of. Concini told her I spoke poorly of her to him."

"No' that it should matter, but did ye?" Angus asked.

"I'm afraid so. It seems she was angry that I questioned the dowry and Concini told me that she made remarks that were complete lies. She knows that my family are all dead and she said she assumed I'd had them poisoned so I would be the sole heir to the family fortune. I was furious and said some unflattering things about the Queen Mother and her family. I told Concini it was something her family was known for, not mine." Angus could see how tense he was, how worried he was about what he had said in anger. "It was a mistake to say what I was thinking, especially to Concini. I should have known he would tell her everything I said and would probably add more."

"I doona ken much about Concini other than he is the Queen Mother's favorite," Edna said.

"He enjoys gossiping and creating problems. If there is a rumor going through the palace it likely came from Concini," Matteo explained. "I have known him for many years. Even when he lived in Rome, he was not above pitting one friend against another with his gossip and lies." He bristled at the thought of it.

Angus didn't like the sounds of that. It seemed no matter what happened with the dowry, there would be a wedding.

"So Marie plans to punish ye. I might be able to fix this, but it may no' be easy."

"I would be most grateful, Madame Campbell," Matteo said.

"There are nae guarantees it will work, but I will give it a try for yer sake as well as Emilie's."

"What will you do?" Matteo asked.

"That will be me little secret." She held a finger up to her lips. "Doona mention me involvement to anyone."

"As you wish," Matteo said.

"If I ken me Edna, everything will work out as it should," Angus assured Matteo.

Matteo clasped his hands in front of his chest. "Let us hope."

～

Marie de Medici and her ladies arrived in the throne room where she took a moment to greet some visitors who'd been patiently waiting along with everyone else. Once she settled onto her throne, she motioned for Matteo to come to her.

Edna and Angus stayed where they were, knowing they would still able to listen in on the conversation.

If the smug look on Marie's face was an omen of what was to come, then things might be about to get worse for Emilie and Robert. "Well, Barbieri, we have searched and searched and there does not seem to be a dowry."

Matteo stiffened his spine and through barely gritted teeth said, "Then we shall not marry."

"You will marry!" Marie commanded. "I have told you that we have information that would place you in a poor light among your peers. It will be sent to Rome where it will be spread far and wide. The church may even choose to excommunicate you." Marie seemed very pleased with herself. The scowl on her face as she waited for a response from Matteo would scare anyone who saw it.

Matteo smartly remained silent. While Edna couldn't see his face, his posture was rigid and his fists were clenched at his sides. She imagined that if he had been able to get a hold of Marie at that moment, he might forget who she was and strangle her.

Marie continued, "The marriage will take place tomorrow. Do not even think of leaving. My guards will be watching you. If you attempt to leave, they will lock you up until it is time for the wedding."

Matteo turned and stormed out of the room followed by the guards as Marie had promised.

"Now what?" Angus asked.

"I have some thoughts, but I will need time to work out a plan." Edna had only one thought in mind that might work. She had to somehow get Concini to recant what he'd told Marie about Matteo. Even then she couldn't be sure Marie would change her mind, especially if she felt it made her look foolish or wrong. It was going to be a challenge, but Edna was determined to see it through.

EMILIE WAITED for Robert in the trees where they always met. She could see him as he strode her way. His dark tresses moved with him as a breeze hit him while he walked. She could hardly wait to be in his arms once again. Before he could reach her, he was stopped by Concino Concini. Emilie didn't care for the man. She was, of course, grateful that he'd agreed to pay off her father's debts, but she didn't trust him. He was always at the center of some trouble happening in the palace, especially where it concerned Marie. He had her ear and the ability to convince her of whatever scandal he had created for his own amusement. Robert spoke with him for some time and then continued to walk her way, breaking into a jog as he approached her.

"What was that all about?" Emilie asked as Robert took her into his arms.

"Concini wondered when Louis would be back from hunting. I'm no' sure why it's any concern of his, but I told him it might be another day or two, especially if the hunt was successful."

"I'm sure the Queen Mother was looking for him," Emilie said.

"Ye're probably right." Robert tucked his nose into her neck. "Ye smell delicious."

His breath tickled her as he kissed his way up her neck to her earlobe. She couldn't help the tiny giggle that escaped her lips. "Robert, perhaps we should walk somewhere outside of the palace. I'm worried someone might see us."

"They've never seen us before, why would today be any different?" he asked, before gently kissing her lips.

Emilie reluctantly pulled away. "You're right. I'm so happy, Robert. Soon we'll be married and have our whole lives before us. Won't that be wonderful?"

Robert caressed her face with his hand before tucking a loose curl behind her ear. "It will be what I have wanted for so long. We'll find a place to live here in Paris. Would ye like that?"

"I would love it. If we're together, I don't care where we live."

"Shall we sit here beneath the trees and enjoy being together?"

Emilie knew exactly what he meant. She lifted her head to look into his beautiful hazel eyes. The mix of green and brown mesmerized her every time she saw him. "Kiss me, please."

It was an order Robert obeyed without hesitation. He captured her lips with his own, kissing her until she was breathless. Letting her go, Emilie watched as he placed an extra plaid he carried with him, on the ground under the trees before coming back to her. He lifted her easily in his arms, placing her atop the plaid. She held her arms out to him as he joined her. Their lips met again and again as Emilie allowed herself to close her eyes and enjoy the feel of his lips on her neck and down to her décolletage. One hand caressed her breast as the other lifted her skirt before moving softly and smoothly to the vee between her legs. Her breathing quickened as his fingers gently caressed her, causing feelings she wanted more of. Emilie was enjoying the pleasure he was bringing her, her hips moving with his hand causing a loud moan to escape her lips. Robert quickly covered her mouth with his, kissing her. Her body was tingling from head to toe. "Robert we mustn't go any further. Someone will hear us."

Robert understood and immediately removed his hands. "We should go now before I can no' stop meself from taking more of ye than I should. We'll be married soon enough and then I'll finish what was started today."

Emilie caught her breath, straightening her gown and then taking his arm. He helped her up, packed up his plaid and with one more quick peck on the lips, they left the palace grounds through a back gate in the garden and headed for the Seine.

"When we have children, will we want to stay in Paris, or should we go somewhere else?" Emilie asked Robert as they strolled along the river path. Her face was hidden by the hood of her cloak, which she held in position with her hands. It wouldn't do for anyone to spy on them as they walked.

"We can go wherever ye wish," Robert said.

"I've never given it much thought before now. I always thought I'd spend my life here in Paris or at my family home." Her life had been very sheltered. At home she was never allowed to wander very far. When she was finally allowed to join Marie as one of her ladies at the palace, Emilie felt it was a turning point in her life. No longer at home under her father's roof there was a feeling of freedom, but still she had someone to answer to. Marie made it clear what her expectations were of her ladies and Emilie, always eager to please, did exactly what was desired by her Queen Mother. It wasn't until she met Robert that she began to sneak away from her duties at the palace.

"We may no' be able to stay in Paris," Robert said. "We could go to Scotland, although we would be dependent on the good graces of me brothers and I'm no' so sure they would be verra happy to see me."

Robert had spoken to her at length about his family and so she understood that it might not be the best situation for them. "Then somewhere else," Emilie said. "Edna will help us."

"They are kind people, but I doona ken how they can help us find a place to live."

Emilie glanced at him in amazement. "They are from the future! Edna said she could take us there. What do you think?" Emilie thought it an exciting prospect.

"It is a thought that intrigues and worries me at the same time. It would no' be familiar to us. It may be the answer or it may be a terrible mistake."

"I hadn't thought of it that way," Emilie said. "Still, I believe that if Edna and Angus, two very good people who want to help us, come from this place, how can it be bad?"

Robert looked back over his shoulder, even going so far as to turn around completely. "I feel as though someone is following us, but I see nae one."

Emilie looked back, being careful to keep her face hidden. "There is no one there."

"It is just a feeling that I have. As Louis' guard, I am always on alert for danger."

"Perhaps we should go back to the palace," Emilie suggested.

"I feel that we have no' settled anything," Robert said.

"If there is no dowry, then we will have time." She peeked at Robert from her hooded cape. "I don't wish to worry about such things. I choose to believe all will be well for us."

"How can ye be so sure?" Robert asked.

Emilie laughed. "I cannot, but I have faith that you and I were meant to be together. That is why the moon heard me and sent Edna to help us."

"Verra well. I will choose to believe as ye do." His eyes danced with amusement as he teased, "All will be well for us because the moon wishes it to be so."

"Do you make fun of me?" Emilie asked, feigning insult. She knew he was teasing her and played along.

"I doona make fun. I love ye, Emilie. I want ye to be me wife more than I've ever wanted anything, and if the moon can make it so, then I am a believer." He brought her hand to his lips, kissing it. It was the happiest Emilie thought that she had ever seen him.

They turned back to the palace focused only on one another, and nothing else.

CHAPTER

# THIRTEEN

"I wonder if anyone has told Emilie that the wedding will still take place?" Edna asked.

"We were no' able to find her or Robert. Perhaps they've heard and decided to run away."

"If that's the case, we'll ken soon enough. In the meantime, I've got something I must do. Do ye think ye could convince Concini to come over here?" Edna asked. The man was across the room waiting for Marie to reappear.

"I'll see what I can do. Ye have a plan?" Angus asked, eyeing her with some concern.

"I do. I'm going to spell him so that he tells me what he's been up to."

"Why doona ye just come with me? It would be easier. Getting him to leave his spot when he's waiting on Marie might no' work."

"Ye're probably right." Edna glanced around the room. No one was paying them any attention and so she took his arm and walked with him to Concini.

"Good day to ye, sir," Angus said as they approached him.

Concini gave a slight nod of his head, acknowledging them, but then looked away.

"Sir, may I ask something of ye?" Edna had to get his attention if the spell were to work.

Concini looked at her with such disdain that it threw Edna off for a brief moment.

"Well, what is it you want?" Concini asked, his impatience showing.

"I just wondered what color yer eyes were." Edna stared into his eyes.

Concini looked at her as if she'd lost her mind for only a moment before he became mesmerized and unable to look away.

Edna worked her magic on him. "Are ye the one behind the betrothal?"

"I am." His voice was without emotion. The spell was working.

"What exactly are ye up to?" Edna asked, knowing that it had to be more than she currently knew.

"I wanted the land," he said.

"Monsieur Toussaint's land?" Edna tried to keep her face impassive so that anyone watching wouldn't be too curious about their conversation.

"Yes."

"Did ye get it?" she asked.

"Yes. When he came to the palace to speak with the Queen Mother I was there. He explained his position and that he wished his daughter to be taken care of."

"Ye mean he told Marie that he was penniless?"

"Yes. She told him she could not help him, but I convinced her that I could with a little help from her. I offered to take care of his debts and find a husband for his daughter. Monsieur Toussaint agreed, of course. I chose Barbieri because I hated him and knew he was more interested in money than a wife. He would do anything to stay in the good graces of the Medici family in Italy. After Toussaint was dead and there were questions about the dowry, which I certainly was not going to pay, Marie became irritated with me. I could not allow her anger to come between us and so I told her Barbieri had cheated her family in his business dealings with them and that he said some unkind things about her. It was quite easy to sway her. She wanted her revenge and so she will make him go through with the marriage."

Edna couldn't believe what she was hearing. "So, Marie kenned about this all along."

"Yes. She did it for me. It cost her nothing at all."

"Ye will undo what ye have done. Ye will tell Marie that Emilie is free to marry whomever she wishes. Ye will tell her that ye have lied to her about Matteo." She then silently placed the thoughts in his head that would work to hopefully change Marie's mind. She then made it imperative that he speak with Marie about Matteo as soon as she arrived. When Edna released him, he turned away. Everything went the way she planned it. He had no recollection that she'd even spoken to him. Angus took her arm and maneuvered them away to a spot where they could see and hear everything that might occur once Marie arrived.

They didn't have to wait long. Marie appeared and Concini was at her side the moment she sat down, whispering in her ear. It took only a moment before she stopped him.

She sat back in her throne with a look of disbelief on her face. "Are you telling me that the things you told me about Barbieri were not true?"

"I was lied to, Marie." He bowed his head as though he were a young lad being chastised by his mother.

"And the things he said to you about me?" she asked.

"I may have exaggerated them a bit."

"What do you mean exaggerated?"

"Do not be angry with me." He lifted his eyes and then quickly glanced back down at the floor. "He never said anything at all."

"I am very disappointed in you, Concino. Why would you tell me lies?"

"I was jealous. I was afraid you would begin to favor Barbieri over me."

"Over you? Why would you think I would favor him over you? I don't even know the man."

"I have always been jealous of him. Please forgive me."

"You are forgiven. It was a mistake on your part. One you shall never repeat. Do you understand me?"

"Yes, Your Highness. I understand."

"Go away. I cannot stand to look at you."

"You wish me to leave?" Concini asked. He appeared quite panic stricken.

"Not forever, you fool. Go. I am angry and it will take me time before I wish to see you again." Marie looked to the side. It was obvious she was punishing him by removing her attention from him.

He bowed to the Queen Mother and left the room appearing quite dejected.

Edna turned toward Angus. "It worked. Now we'll have to see what she does next."

"Hopefully she releases Matteo from the betrothal," Angus said.

"Only time will tell. Me only concern now is that as the Queen Mother she may no' wish to admit she was wrong. If that is the case, we are back where we started."

"I wonder where Matteo is?" Angus asked. "I thought he'd be here this morning."

"Maybe we should go look for him," Edna said. "We can tell him what happened with Concini."

"Ye'll no' tell him about yer spell," Angus said.

"Doona worry. I willnae mention me part in it at all."

"Let's see if he's in the garden," Angus said. "He enjoys sunning himself on one of the benches."

"Ye ken a lot more about him than I do," Edna said.

"We've become friends in the short time we've known each other."

"Lead the way then," Edna said, allowing Angus to guide her outside into the sunshine.

They were walking down the center aisleway when something caught Edna's eye at the far end of the garden. "Look," she said, pointing towards two figures entering the garden from the rear gate. The man headed for the stables and the woman for the palace. "It's Robert and Emilie."

"So it is," Angus said.

"I wonder where those two love birds have been?" Edna couldn't help but smile. "Isnae love wonderful?"

"From me experience, aye, it is," Angus said, raising Edna's hand to his lips. "It is the most wonderful thing in the whole wide world because I have ye."

"Angus, ye're such a sweet talker," Edna said.

"It's the truth. Our love has been the most important thing in me life. I cannae imagine how I would have turned out without ye."

"Ye'd still be a braw, handsome man, but fate was good to us and we doona have to imagine our lives without each other."

Edna leaned into Angus, and he placed his arm around her shoulder as they continued their walk.

"Look, there's Matteo," Angus said.

It seemed he was coming from the same area where Robert and Emilie had been.

"Matteo," Angus said, as he was about to pass them.

"I have news for the Queen Mother," Matteo said. "Excuse me if I don't stop to speak with you." He hurried past them.

Edna grabbed Angus by the arm and rushed to follow. He was far from the serene and composed gentleman they'd come to know. Matteo Barbieri was fuming. He marched into the throne room like a man possessed, nostrils flared and face reddened.

"He must be upset that the wedding is still on," Edna whispered to Angus.

He brushed past several people without a word and headed

straight for Marie. "I must speak with you, Your Highness." His voice shook with anger.

"What now?" Marie seemed disinclined to let him speak, but after a moment seemed to think better of ignoring him and allowed it.

Matteo appeared to take a moment to collect himself and then clearing his throat, proceeded in a more rational tone of voice. "I have just witnessed something unspeakable."

Marie sat up a bit taller in her throne. He definitely had her attention now. "Go on."

"I understand that you wanted me to marry Emilie Toussaint and I was willing to do as you commanded, but I have just witnessed her in the arms of another man. I have been cuckolded. I cannot and will not marry her." It was apparent he was adamant and would not back down.

"Who is the man she was with?" Marie asked, her voice raised in outrage was now loud enough for all present in the throne room to hear.

Concini appeared out of nowhere at Matteo's side. He ignored the look Marie was giving him. "I have seen it as well, Your Highness. The man is your son's guard."

"Robert MacMillan." It wasn't a question, but a statement of what she knew to be a fact.

"Yes, Your Highness," Concini said.

"I want him gone!" she shouted. "I knew I should have sent him away. As luck would have it, Louis is not here. He will not be able to stop me. Find MacMillan and have him escorted from the palace. I want him on a boat back to Scotland immediately."

Concini hurried off to do her bidding, obviously eager to please her and be back in her good graces.

"If I had known, I would not have insisted you marry her." She looked down her nose at him, either unable or unwilling to make an apology. "It appears you've gotten your wish. There will be no marriage. You may go."

"I will be on my way back to Rome then." Matteo straightened his frock and headed for the door.

"I'm going to go speak with him," Angus said.

Edna took hold of his arm. "No' yet."

Marie was speaking again in a commanding tone. "Find Emilie Toussaint and bring her here to me."

Marie's ladies-in-waiting hurried out of the room.

"This isnae quite what we wanted, but it has given Marie the perfect excuse to change her mind about the marriage," Edna said. "Angus, I'd rather ye follow Robert and make sure he doesnae get on that ship. I'll stay here and see what lies in store for Emilie."

"Ye're right. I'll be sorry no' to say goodbye to Matteo, but it's more important that I follow Robert."

ANGUS RUSHED to the stables where he'd seen Robert headed earlier. One of the footmen saw him coming and ran to get his horse.

"Angus," Robert was astride his gelding. "Are ye joining me?"

"Robert there's something ye should ken."

"Ye seem serious. Is there trouble?"

"Aye. The Queen Mother has ordered ye to be taken to a ship bound for Scotland."

Before Robert could say another thing, the Queen Mother's guard arrived along with Concini.

"You are under arrest Robert MacMillan." Concini's smug appearance belied the fact that he'd just been berated by the Queen Mother.

Robert glanced at Angus and then back to the guards. "I willnae fight ye."

Angus realized there was no place for them to go. Escaping the garden would be difficult if not impossible and so Robert had made the right call to go along with them. Angus silently let Robert know with a look and a nod of his head, that he was with him.

"Bind his hands," Concini ordered.

Robert dismounted while the guards tied his hands and then helped him mount his horse once more. They seemed saddened to do so. These were men who were Robert's friends and fellow guards.

"We are bound for Le Havre. Get your horses ready." Concini motioned for one of the footmen who brought a horse all saddled for him to ride. He mounted and looked at Robert. "The Queen Mother has wanted you gone for some time now, but Louis always got in the way. She now has good reason to send you back where you came from."

"What good reason?" Robert asked.

"You have been with the woman who was to be Comte Matteo Barbieri's wife. You are now banished from court. Luckily, Louis is away and will not interfere."

Angus stayed silent. He intended on making the journey with them and if an opportunity presented itself, he would free Robert. He was sure Concini would make a mistake somewhere along the way.

Edna knew where they were headed and if she was able, she would meet them. Hopefully she would have Emilie with her. Then decisions would need to be made, but for now he would follow along a short distance behind them. He would be at the ready should Robert need him.

EMILIE WAS SEATED in her favorite spot, enjoying the fresh air for a few moments longer before going back inside. Feeling happier than she had in some time, she thought about Robert and about their time together this afternoon. It was the first time that they'd felt able to begin making plans for their life together. She knew it wasn't what her father had wanted for her, but she also thought that if he knew how happy Robert made her, he would approve.

The sound of skirts swishing hurriedly towards her caught her attention. Looking up, she saw the other ladies-of-the-court heading her way. She stood, wondering what was wrong.

"Emilie," Antoinette, one of the ladies said. "We have found you."

"What's wrong?" Emilie asked.

"The Queen Mother is angry. She wishes to see you right away."

"Why? What is it?"

"I would rather not say. It is not my place."

"I'll be right there."

"You must come with us, now."

A knot formed in the pit of Emilie's stomach. Something about this felt ominous. She couldn't imagine what it would be other than something to do with her betrothal. Perhaps they hadn't found the dowry and Marie was angry about that. If that were the case, Emilie would happily deal with Marie's anger. It would mean that she was free to marry Robert and start a new life with him. From the look on Antoinette's face though, she thought it might be something more, but what? There was no way to know until she stood before the Queen Mother.

The ladies escorted her to the palace, but left Emilie to enter the throne room on her own. Approaching Marie, Emilie curtsied before the Queen Mother and stayed in position until she was spoken to.

"Look at me," Marie commanded.

"Your Highness," Emilie said, as she raised her eyes.

Marie stared at her for what seemed an eternity before she spoke. "Emilie Toussaint, I am very unhappy. Do you know why?"

"Is it because I have no dowry?" Emilie asked, seeming puzzled.

"There is no dowry, but no that is not the reason. It is because you went behind my back. You promised me you would not resist your betrothal any longer and yet you continued to have an affair with Robert MacMillan." She eyed Emilie with disgust. "I have treated you like a daughter and this is the way you repay me?"

Emilie could hardly speak. She was being accused of something she hadn't done. Yes, she had kissed Robert many times, but that was as far as it ever went. She opened her mouth, but before she could utter a word in her defense, Marie held up her hand and then stood and walked to stand in front of Emilie. She was an intimidating woman on a good day, but today, being the object of her disdain was terrifying.

"You will not speak. I have heard enough. Many people have seen you with him. There is nothing more I can do for you here in my palace. You will be banished to the Abbey Port-Royal Des Champs."

"The convent?" Emilie was being shamed by the Queen Mother and being sent to a place where she would feel even more shame. At least she would not have to stay there forever. Robert would find her and all would be well once again. It would only be for a short while and then she would be married and happy.

"I will have a letter written to the abbess telling her why you are being sent to her. She will decide what penance needs to be done."

"What of Robert?" Emilie thought there may still be a possibility Marie would allow her to leave with Robert and all would be well.

"He has been sent back to Scotland, and will never return to France. You will never see him again."

Emilie fell to her knees. Her heart was broken. She would never see him again. She had been so happy just a short while ago and now her life was in ruins. If she had run away with Robert instead of waiting to hear about the dowry they would be far away by now, but instead her dreams were shattered. Two of Marie's guards lifted her from the floor by her arms and took her away.

CHAPTER

# FOURTEEN

Edna had been ushered out of the throne room along with everyone else who had been waiting to see Marie. The hallway was crowded with those who'd been sent out. They gathered around the doors waiting for them to open once again. In such close quarters it became warm very quickly. Fans were produced by the ladies to ease oppressive body heat emanating from the crowd. Someone stepped on the back of Edna's dress yanking her backwards as she tried to move closer to the door. A rumble of whispers made it impossible to hear anything that was going on inside through the thick wooden doors. She would have to wait along with everyone else.

When the doors were finally opened again, Edna was pushed from behind as she entered the room. A rush of swirling skirts blew past her as the throne room filled with those anxious to gossip about what was happening. Hoping to see Emilie, Edna turned about the room but she wasn't there. Marie and her guards were still present although occupied with those now streaming in to speak with the queen.

"Where is Emilie?" she asked one of Marie's ladies.

"She has been taken away."

"Where?" Edna didn't like this. She had to find her. "Where have they taken her?"

"Perhaps Antoinette knows."

"Who is Antoinette?"

"She is there speaking with the Queen Mother." She pointed to a young woman who was just stepping away from Marie's side.

Edna followed her as she left the room and grabbed her arm.

"What do you want?" the woman asked, seeming frightened and upset.

"I'm sorry." Edna quickly released her arm realizing she'd startled her. "Are ye Antoinette?"

She nodded her head.

"I need to find Emilie. Do ye ken where they've taken her?"

"She is being taken to the convent," she said, dabbing her eyes with a handkerchief. "Poor, sweet Emilie."

"Oh, no! Where is this convent?" Edna asked. Under normal circumstances, Edna would have comforted Antoinette, but this was turning into an emergency situation. She had to know exactly where Emilie was going.

"Port-Royal Abbey," the woman said.

Edna patted the woman's hand. "Thank ye."

This was not the way she'd expected things to go. Edna had to find Angus and hoped that he had been able to get to Robert before the ship left for Scotland. She ran from the palace, causing those she passed to appear aghast at her behavior. Edna entered the courtyard just as Louis and his entourage rode in.

Waving her arms to get his attention, Edna hurried to Louis as he dismounted his horse. One of Louis men stepped between Edna and the young king obviously to protect him from what he saw as a possible threat. Out of breath and realizing her mistake, Edna stopped. "I mean nae harm. I must speak with the king."

The guard did not budge.

"Allow her to speak," Louis said, shoving the man out of the way.

"Yer Highness, Robert MacMillan has been banished from court along with Emilie Toussaint." She hoped that this news would be upsetting enough to Louis that he would be spurred into action.

"This cannot be true. Where has he gone and why?" Louis didn't seem to believe what she was telling him.

"He has been taken to a ship that will head for Scotland. Emilie is on her way to a convent."

"My mother has outdone herself." He mounted his horse once again. "I will find him."

Before he could urge his horse forward, Edna stopped him. "May I join ye, Yer Highness? I believe me husband Angus Campbell may be with them." she asked.

"I have ridden with your husband. He is an excellent horseman."

"He is and he cares a great deal about Robert. He wanted to be sure he would be safe and that he wouldnae board that boat."

He motioned to one of his men. "Give the lady your horse."

The man did as instructed and then gave Edna a leg up onto the horse, which she was grateful for. Ordinarily she would need no help at all, but in the voluminous dress she now wore, climbing up into the saddle would have been amusing, to say the least, for those standing around watching them. "Thank ye. Ye are most kind." The saddle dictated that she ride astride as the men did, which took some maneuvering as she tucked her dress in around her legs and pulled it out from beneath her seat so that it flowed back and over the horse's rump. Satisfied, she sat up tall and nodded to Louis.

Once he seemed sure that Edna was ready to ride they headed off. "Where will we be going?" she asked.

"Le Havre. They will be on their way there. If they are not too far ahead, we may catch them." Louis led his men with Edna at his side. Taking the horses up to a canter, they left the courtyard and headed off to find Robert and Angus.

"Will you be able to hold on if we go faster?" Louis asked.

Edna was surprised by his concern for her, but she was a capable rider and could withstand a gallop. "Of course."

"Ah, like your husband. You are good on a horse." Louis signaled to his men and they sped off, leaving Paris behind and heading for the open sea. "Le Havre is more than a day's ride," he shouted over the sounds of the galloping horses. "It is doubtful that the guards who took Robert would have gotten very far."

Edna's only worry at the moment was whether Angus had managed to get hold of a horse so he could keep up with them. Talking at the speed they were going was difficult, but Edna somehow managed to do it. "I believe Concino Concini is leading them," she shouted. Edna mentioned this only because it might be something Louis should know.

Louis slowed his horse to a trot and the others followed his lead. "We do not need to hurry then. Concini is not a gifted rider. He is at his best when he has my mother's ear and is filling it with lies."

"Ye doona like him," Edna observed.

Louis laughed at this. "I despise him. He is worthless. I do not understand my mother's fascination with him."

"Perhaps he is entertaining," Edna suggested.

"Perhaps. My mother's interests are limited to political intrigue and I will tell you that she does not excel at this." He chuckled, obviously finding his own thoughts on his mother amusing.

"She doesnae ride with ye?" Edna asked, hoping to get more of an understanding of his relationship with his mother.

"No. She prefers her carriage. We have little in common other than the throne. She is the regent for the time being, but I am about to come of age and will take my rightful place on the throne when I do."

Historically, it wasn't always a good thing to be a king or queen. They oftentimes found themselves jailed or murdered by those who wished to take their place or didn't agree with their politics or religion. Edna knew this would not be Louis' fate. He would die of natural causes. He would not be an old man, but at least he would not die at the hands of another. She glanced at him. It was a strange thing to know another person's fate. Seeing him now as a thirteen-year-old boy, she understood that he would have to grow up fast. He was already showing signs of being a mature young man who could take decisive actions that would affect not only himself but his kingdom. She knew from history that unfortunately his relationship with his mother would always be strained. Edna was not here to fix history, so she would mind her own business and focus on Robert and Emilie. They were her only reason for being here.

After what must have been hours in the saddle, they spied riders up ahead of them.

"There they are," Louis said. As they approached, he called out, "You there! Stop!"

The men looked back and recognizing Louis, did as he'd ordered.

"Your Highness," Concini, who was leading the group, doffed his hat and bowed his head. The other's followed suit.

"Robert, I've come to rescue you." Louis said, a crooked grin on his lips.

Robert returned the grin with one of his own. "I kenned I could count on ye."

Much to Edna's relief, Angus was with them and right beside Robert. How he'd convinced Concini to let him join them was something she'd ask him later.

"Your Highness, your mother has requested we take this man to Le Havre so he may return to his homeland." Concini said.

"That is not what he wishes and it is certainly not what I wish." Louis stared at Concini with obvious disdain.

"Your mother will not be happy," Concini said, appearing to believe that Louis would be put in his place by this pronouncement.

"It is not my mother's happiness I am concerned with. Robert is my guard and I want him at the palace. You will do as I have commanded. Do you understand?"

"As you wish," Concini bowed his head to Louis.

"Untie his hands," Louis ordered.

Concini motioned to the man closest to Robert who did as he had been ordered.

Now that he was free, Robert stretched his arms high overhead before bringing them back down and rubbing his wrists.

Edna could certainly sympathize. Riding for hours without her hands tied was giving her aches and pains she hadn't experienced since, well, since the last time she'd ridden this much.

"We will return to the palace," Louis motioned the men with his arm to turn their horses for home.

The men all started moving in that direction.

"Wait!" Edna shouted. "Emilie has been taken to a convent."

Robert stopped his horse, exchanging a worried glance with Edna and then turning to Louis. "I must get to her, Louis," Robert said. "Ye ken that I love her and ye've told me more than once that ye want me to be happy."

Louis took a moment before speaking. "Then go. You will be together after all. I understand the palace is not a place you will wish to be."

"Thank ye for this," Robert said, smiling warmly at Louis. The two clasped hands in a handshake. It would undoubtedly be the last time they would see each other.

"You have been a good friend to me. I do not wish to give you up, but as you say, I want you to be happy. Also, it will make my mother quite angry to hear what I have done." Louis laughed as he motioned to the men as they trotted off towards Paris.

"Do we ken how to get to this convent?" Angus asked.

"I'm hoping Robert does."

"If it's Port-Royal, it's in the Valley of Chevreuse. It is about a half day's ride from here."

"That's exactly where she is. We should get started then," Edna said.

As the three of them rode towards Chevreuse, Edna was relieved that she now had Robert with her. Once they had Emilie they would have to decide what was next. She had some thoughts on the subject, but she would wait to hear what Robert and Emilie wanted for themselves.

~

"WE WILL MAKE camp here for the night," Robert said, hopping down from his horse.

Angus followed suit before lifting Edna from the saddle.

"Are ye sure ye doona wish to continue?" Edna asked.

"I am quite sure, as it is already too dark to ride safely. It has been a long day and we all need our rest."

Edna knew he was doing this on her behalf and was grateful. "We'll get started early tomorrow morning then."

"Aye. Emilie will be safe at the convent until we arrive."

"I couldnae agree more," Angus said.

Edna did some stretching to help alleviate the stiffness she was feeling in her back and neck. When she stopped, Angus was right there to rub her shoulders. "Thank ye, love."

"Ye'll feel it more tomorrow. We should get a good night's sleep if possible."

They found a spot in the field they'd been riding through where they could stomp down the grass, making a little nest for themselves. Robert removed plaids from his saddle bag and laid them out on the ground.

"Ye're certainly prepared," Edna noted.

"Always," Robert replied.

They would use their saddles for pillows. And while Edna and Angus arranged everything so the three of them would be as comfortable as possible, Robert made a small fire to keep them warm.

Angus removed something wrapped in paper from his saddle bag.

"What have ye got there?" Edna asked.

"I stopped at the baker's as we were leaving the city. I kenned I could catch up with them and assumed food might be something we'd need, so I picked up some bread and candied chestnuts." He handed the bag to Edna.

"Angus, ye are a blessing."

"And doona forget genius," he teased.

"How could I?" she tipped her head and hoped that her smile showed him how much she loved him.

They sat around the fire and shared the bread and chestnuts. Angus also had pouches of wine that he'd worn across his body while they rode.

"This is lovely," Edna said, sipping some of the wine. "The only thing that could make it more perfect would be if Emilie were here with us."

"She would enjoy this," Robert said.

"Are ye feeling that ye may finally get what ye've wanted all along?" Edna asked.

"I doona wish to tempt fate, but aye. To have Emilie as me wife is all I've thought about since I first set eyes on her. It will make me life complete." His voice was quiet, almost wistful and in the light of the fire, Edna could see Robert smile softly.

"I doona believe in tempting fate either, but I have a good feeling that all yer dreams will come true." Edna snuggled up against Angus, enjoying the crackle of the fire and the distinctive sound of crickets nearby.

"If ye doona mind, I think I'll sleep now." Robert reclined, placing his head on his saddle.

"Of course," Angus said. "I will keep first watch."

"I'll join ye, if ye doona mind," Edna said.

"Naething would make me happier." Angus kissed the top of her head as she leaned into him.

"It looks like we did it, Angus," Edna whispered.

"We're no' there yet, love."

"I ken, but we've gotten Emilie out of her marriage contract and both of them out of the palace."

"True, but in actual fact, it seems they did both of those things without our help."

"Ye're right. I cannae take credit for that, but we are helping them to get away and to make plans for their life together."

"We'll see how things go tomorrow at the convent." Angus, it seemed, didn't want to tempt fate any more than Edna or Robert.

"It should be an easy thing to have her released from the convent." Edna couldn't imagine they would want to keep Emilie there once they understood that love was at stake. The nuns certainly wouldn't stand in the way of that.

The night grew even quieter. Angus stoked the fire, adding more wood to keep it going. In a few hours they would be on their way to Port-Royal Abbey and Edna and Angus would be closer to going back home.

# FIFTEEN

Emilie was taken to Abbey Port-Royal Des Champs by Marie de Medici's guards. The journey had been uncomfortable for Emilie as the carriage she was in bounced along the roadway, hurrying to get to the convent. Once there, the men were relieved of their duties by the Abbess Arnould, who took over care of Emilie.

Seated in her office, the abbess read the note she'd received from Marie de Medici. She shook her head as she read and looked at Emilie with what was a mixture of pity and disapproval.

"It seems you have ruined yourself in the eyes of the Queen Mother and she wishes you to stay here and repent for your sins." She gazed at Emilie over the top of the note.

"I have not sinned," Emilie said. "The Queen Mother is mistaken."

"The Queen Mother is never mistaken. You must know that. It is disrespectful to think otherwise."

Emilie would have normally bowed her head and done as she was told, but this wasn't one of those times. "You must let me leave. I have to find the man I am to marry."

"The man you were to marry didn't want you. That is why you are here. It says so in the note." The abbess placed the note on her desk and gazed at Emilie.

"There is another man. A man I love with all my heart. We wish to be together." Emilie knew she must sound frantic, because she was. She had to get to Robert before they sent him away from her for good.

"Perhaps you should have thought of that before you gave yourself to him." There was much disapproval showing on the face of the abbess. She wrinkled her nose as if she had just smelled something foul.

"But I haven't. Will no one listen to me?" Emilie was distraught and could see she was getting nowhere with the abbess. There was no point in arguing. "How long must I stay here?"

"That will be determined by your behavior. You have made mistakes and that is why you are here. Your father is dead, you have no money, no family and now you are a fallen woman. There is every possibility you will want to stay with us even when you are allowed to leave."

Emilie couldn't imagine that ever happening. She was already planning her escape. It was a long way back to Paris and an even longer way to Scotland, but she would find Robert if it was the last thing she ever did.

"I will show you to your room." The abbess placed her hands on her desk, pushing herself up to stand. Emilie followed her outside and then up a set of stairs that led to a main hall. From there another set of stairs took them to the room Emilie would reside in. It was tiny with just enough room for a small bed, side table and window. A single candle was set on the table.

"Use it wisely," the abbess said of the candle. "It is meant to last you three days before it is replaced."

Emilie could see she'd be spending a lot of time in the dark.

"Each morning as the sun rises, the bells will ring, calling you to matins. You will be expected to be there."

"And if I'm not?" Emilie asked.

"You will be punished. There is no reason for you to miss it. Chores are done immediately after and then we have a simple breakfast. The rest of the morning will be spent in contemplation."

Emilie didn't respond. She didn't care what the abbess was saying because as soon as she could, she would run away. If there was a way out, she would find it. She was determined not to let these circumstances prevent her from having the life she wanted. The life she'd been expecting to have with Robert.

"May I explore the grounds?" Emilie asked.

"Of course. You will find the gates are locked to keep unwanted guests out and those who'd choose to leave locked in."

"Do people try to get in or out often?" Emilie asked, trying to sound more concerned than curious.

"It has happened. Don't worry. You are well-protected while you are here."

"Thank you." There was no benefit in being difficult with the abbess. Emilie thought it would be better to have the Abbess on her side and so she vowed she would not give any cause for suspicion.

"I will leave you. If you have any questions, you know where to find me." As the abbess began to close the door behind her, she looked Emilie over from head to toe. "We'll see to your clothing once you have settled in."

Emilie sat on the bed. The mattress was thin and covered with one wool blanket to keep her warm. It was hard to believe that she'd gone from the privileged life of a lady-in-waiting to a nunnery where she was being treated like a criminal. How life had changed in just one day.

She stood to gaze out the small window her room had been afforded. Emilie's thoughts of climbing out were dashed. First of all, the window itself was too narrow and secondly, it was on an upper floor. Still, it gave her a vantage point of the world outside of the convent, which was set in the countryside and surrounded by trees and fields of green. It was breathtakingly beautiful, but Emilie did not feel she would be enjoying the view much longer.

Heading for the door, she looked around the room one more time before leaving to explore the grounds of the convent. The abbess said that everything was locked, so Emilie felt she would need to be clever to find a way out of this prison. At the bottom of the stairs, she decided to head away from the office where she'd met the abbess and walk the path that wound its way along the side of the building. Several women, all dressed in matching drab dresses, walked along nearby. Some looked at her with curiosity and others with pity. None of them seemed capable of returning the smile Emilie bestowed upon them. She wondered if she'd be forced to wear the same dull gray clothing she was seeing on everyone she passed. The long shapeless tunic covered them from neck to feet. Their hair was covered by a matching veil, leaving their faces exposed.

Looking down at her pretty blue gown, Emilie dreaded the thought of losing it only to be replaced by what she'd seen. Once in conversation with the women at the palace, they'd laughed as they discussed the nuns clothing and that their hair had to be cut short. Emilie touched her hair, which was quite long, but always worn up except at night when it was plaited for sleep. She shuddered at the thought of losing her beautiful hair.

As Emilie wandered further from the front of the abbey, she came upon one of the gates that would lead to the exterior. She moved closer, examining the lock which was securely set in place. She would need a key to unlock it.

"The abbess is the only one who holds the keys." A thin and pale young woman was standing beside her, which surprised Emilie so much so that she jumped. "I'm sorry. I didn't mean to scare you."

"Where did you come from?" Emilie asked.

"I've been following you. Most of us are here of our own free will, but those who are not generally look for ways out. I imagine you're one of them." Unlike the others, she smiled warmly at Emilie.

"I was just curious." Emilie did her best to sound convincing. The last thing she wanted to do was alert the nuns to her search for escape routes.

"Why are you here?" the woman asked.

"My name is Emilie Toussaint," Emilie said, ignoring her question and still uneasy about being seen. "You are?"

"Sister Therese." She wore the same drab clothing the other nuns donned, but there was a sweet innocence about her which put Emilie more at ease.

Emilie decided it was best to befriend Sister Therese. Having an ally in the convent could be a good thing. "I'm happy to meet you."

"You're avoiding my question. Why are you here?" Sister Therese tipped her head and though her questions were pointed, it seemed she was just curious.

Deciding honesty was the best policy, especially here at the convent, Emilie said, "I'm not really sure. I was supposed to be married today and then I was accused of something I didn't do."

"Did it involve a man?" the nun asked, seeming quite interested.

"Yes. It did."

Sister Therese's eyes lit up as she clasped her hands beneath her chin. "Was he handsome?"

"I don't see why that matters. Handsome or not, nothing happened between us, but I was not believed." Emilie wanted to set the record straight. The last thing she wanted was for the nuns of the abbey to believe she had given herself to anyone.

"Women never are. That is why there are so many of us here." Sister Therese cast her eyes downward, her voice taking on a sad tone.

"Are you here because you want to be?" Emilie asked.

Sister Therese took her time answering. She seemed to be thinking about what she might say. "I did not wish to be here at first, but now I am content to stay."

"The abbess said it might be that way for me as well." Emilie didn't really believe that and she had no intention of finding out.

Sister Therese looked her up and down from head to toe. "You are very pretty and have such a beautiful gown. It would be a shame for you to be stuck here for the rest of your life."

Emilie thought Sister Therese odd. She seemed friendly enough, but this last comment and the way she was gazing at her gave Emilie an uncomfortable feeling. "You don't think you are stuck here?"

"My life outside of these walls was not desirable. Here I have a bed to sleep in and food to eat. No harm will come to me here."

"Were you harmed before you came here?" Emilie wondered what may have happened to her.

Sister Therese appeared distressed by this question as she looked away from Emilie.

"I'm sorry. I didn't mean to upset you," Emilie said.

"I do not wish to speak of it," the nun said through gritted teeth.

Emilie glanced at the locked gate one more time and sighed. She was about to walk away in search of another way out when Sister Therese grabbed her arm, stopping her.

"I can help you."

"Help me?" Emilie asked, prying her arm away.

"I know you do not wish to be here. Why else would you be looking for a way to escape?"

"I'm not. I just wanted to be sure no one could get in," Emilie lied. What if Sister Therese told the abbess? She'd be in more trouble than she was now, she was sure of it.

A short, cynical laugh escaped Sister Therese. "I will help you," she insisted. "Meet me here tonight after everyone has gone to bed. Leave your candle in your room."

"But it will be dark. How will I see to find you?"

"The moon will light your way." Sister Therese left her without another word.

Emilie wasn't sure she could trust the woman. She seemed eager to help, but why? Emilie had never been suspicious. She'd never felt the need to be. Her life had been quiet and predictable. Those around her were meant to protect her, not lie to her. That was not the case any longer. Someone had betrayed her and she wasn't sure who or why. What did she have to lose? Wishing on the moon had brought Edna and Angus to help her. That same moon would guide her to freedom tonight. If Sister Therese was able to get her out of here, it would be worth it. If she was caught, Emilie would find another way.

AFTER EVENING PRAYERS, each of the nuns went straight to their rooms, closing their doors behind them. Emilie did the same and waited until the moon was high. Peeking from her window, she saw what appeared to be lantern light in the distance. Doubt about what was about to happen crept into her mind. She'd never done anything like this before. Life for Emilie had been sheltered and there was no need for her to take risks. That was ending tonight. Getting to Robert was the main objective. If she kept the thought of him ever present, there was no doubt in her mind that she could do this.

Wrapping herself in her cloak, Emilie silently opened the door to her room. It took a minute for her eyes to adjust to the darkness before she headed down the stairs, being careful not to make a sound. Sister Therese had been right. The moon lit her path all the way to the gate where no one was waiting for her. Emilie paced back and forth for an interminable amount of time, or at least it seemed to be to Emilie. She began to wonder if Sister Therese had meant what she'd said. Her eyes peered into the darkness and saw no one. Turning to the gate she tried the latch and was surprised that it swung open. Emilie hurried through, and was about to run when the strong smell of tobacco and sweat alerted her that she was not alone.

Her heart thumped loudly in her chest as a large hand covered her mouth and an arm wrapped around her waist, lifting her from the ground and placing her atop a horse. She felt the man mounting the horse and sitting behind her as he held her close around the waist.

"Who are you?" she managed to squeak out as he loosened his hand. Fear coursed through her body and she shook uncontrollably.

She should cry out for help, but the man would be angry and possibly hurt her. Besides, she wasn't sure she would be heard or that anyone in the convent would even care enough to rescue her. The man behind her was twice her size with a gruff, cold voice that frightened her when he spoke.

"It doesn't matter who I am." He clucked to the horse and it began to walk. "Thank you, Sister Therese."

"Goodbye Emilie," Sister Therese said from somewhere in the shadows. "Good luck in your new life."

"Where are you taking me?" Emilie asked. There was no point in looking around. There was nothing to see. The moon that had guided her to the gate was now hidden behind clouds, leaving the surrounding area so dark that she could barely see the horse she was riding atop.

"To meet your new husband," the man said.

"I don't understand." She wondered if this man was taking her to meet Robert.

"You don't need to understand. I paid Sister Therese for her services and I will collect my payment when I deliver you to your husband."

"But I don't want a husband." She understood now that she was not going to meet Robert. Instead, something unspeakable awaited her.

"That is not my concern. You will do as you're told. Do not even think about trying to escape." A low chuckle rumbled through his chest.

"What is the point in fighting? You are obviously stronger than I." Emilie was resigned to staying where she was. She would hope for a chance to escape or to be rescued, although that seemed unlikely.

"You are a very smart young lady. I'd hate to have to tie you up as I've done with others before you." A sinister whisper in her ear sent a shiver through her.

"You do this often?" Emilie did her best to quell the shakiness in her voice.

"No. Only when the opportunity arises."

Emilie wasn't sure how she would get herself out of this mess. Perhaps in the light of day it would be easier for her to get the attention of a passerby.

"You will have a busy day of travel tomorrow."

"Where am I traveling to?" she asked.

"A boat will meet me along the river. I will hand you over to them get my payment and be on my way. I don't know where you go from there."

"You can't give me any more information than that?"

"I'm afraid it's all I know. I do not have any names if that's what you're thinking. You may lean against me to sleep if you wish."

Sleeping atop a horse would be impossible even if she thought she could, and the last thing she wanted to do was to lean into the man behind her. She held herself stiffly upright to avoid any such contact. Her life was in a downward spiral from which there seemed no escape. It terrified her to know that she was being sold to someone to be their wife. If they couldn't get a wife the way most men did, then what was the reason? The sick feeling in the pit of her belly lingered through the night. As light began to filter through the clouds Emilie couldn't help but think this had to be a bad dream, but she soon found that it was not.

EDNA, Angus and Robert arrived at the Port-Royal Abbey the following morning. They didn't have far to go from their campsite, arriving at the abbey in good time.

"Hopefully they dinna turn her into a nun overnight," Edna said with a laugh.

Robert was a bit more serious. "Do ye believe they would?"

"Of course no'. She only just arrived," Edna assured him.

They dismounted their horses, leaving them to graze on the lush grasses of the abbey.

Finding the gate latched from the inside, Angus rang a bell that was hung nearby. "Hello!"

A moment later the gate opened and they were greeted by a young nun. "Yes. What can I do for you?"

"We're looking for a young lady who may have arrived here yesterday."

"Just a moment please." She disappeared through the gate, closing it behind her.

"They seem overly cautious, doona ye think?" Edna said.

The gate opened again and they were ushered in. "This way."

The nun led them to an office where the abbess was seated behind her desk. "You are looking for Emilie Toussaint, is that correct?"

"Aye, that's right," Edna said.

"She is not here," the abbess said.

"What do ye mean? She must have arrived yesterday."

"She did, but she escaped through an unlocked gate."

"How long ago was that?" Robert asked, his voice filled with worry.

"Sometime after evening prayers."

"She couldnae have gone far," Edna said. "She's on foot."

"Someone met her at the gate and took her away. One of our nuns was nearby at the time and saw them. I assumed it was the man she said she was to marry."

"That isnae possible. I am the man she was to marry," Robert said.

The abbess seemed quite confused by this, which made Edna more uneasy than she already was.

"Who could it be?" Angus asked. "She wouldnae ken anyone all the way out here."

"May we speak with the nun who saw them?" Edna asked. Something was off here and she intended to get to the bottom of it.

"If you wait here, I'll get her for you." The abbess left them alone in her office.

"I doona like this," Robert said, pacing the room. "She could be miles ahead of us by now."

"I cannae imagine she would go with someone on her own. She would ken that to be dangerous," Edna said.

"If she was desperate enough, she may have been willing to take the risk," Angus added.

The abbess returned with a young nun who seemed determined to hide behind the abbess.

"This is Sister Therese," the abbess introduced the nun to them, moving out of the way so she could be seen.

Edna immediately noticed that she was quite nervous and wondered if they'd get anything out of her with the abbess standing by.

"May we speak with her alone?" Edna asked.

"Of course. I'll be nearby if you need me." The abbess headed back out the door.

"Thank ye for yer help." Edna called after her before turning to the young nun. "Sister Therese, I am told ye saw Emilie leaving last night."

"Yes, Madame, I did. She left with a man on horseback." Sister Therese glanced back and forth between Angus and Robert, seeming very wary of them.

"Do ye ken which direction they were headed?" Robert asked.

"I'm not sure. I didn't see which direction they went."

"I think ye ken more than ye're saying," Edna said. She concentrated on Sister Therese, looking into her eyes and using her witchcraft to loosen her tongue.

"The man pays me when someone comes to the convent that would make a good wife. He brings them to the river where they board a boat. I don't know where they go from there."

"So ye sold Emilie to a stranger." Robert's voice rose with enough fury to send the abbess hurrying into the room.

"He is not a stranger to me," Sister Therese said. "His name is Marc Allard."

"Is everything all right?" The abbess glanced around the room, her gaze landing on Sister Therese. "I heard yelling."

"Sister Therese is the culprit here," Robert said, as he pounded the desk with a closed fist.

"What do you mean?" The abbess seemed baffled to hear this.

"She has been selling women to a man named Marc Allard. She sold Emilie to him last night."

"Sister Therese, is this true?" the abbess asked.

Still under Edna's spell, Sister Therese said, "Yes. It is true."

"We should go. The sooner we get started, the sooner we'll find her. We've got to get to her before she boards the boat." Robert was out the door and running towards the horses.

Edna released Sister Therese from her spell and gazed at the abbess. "Can we trust ye to take care of this?"

"Rest assured this will never happen again." She glared at Sister Therese. "She will be punished for what she has done."

Edna nodded her gratitude and grabbing Angus by the hand, ran after Robert.

"Doona worry, Robert. We'll find her," Edna said.

The three rode off at a gallop. Robert seemed to know where they should go and so Edna and Angus followed his lead.

Exhausted from yesterday's travel, Edna's magic came to the rescue, giving them the energy they and their horses needed to continue on at a breakneck pace. After several hours in the saddle they could see the river up ahead.

"There it is!" Robert said, guiding them towards the shoreline. Riding along the banks of the river they saw a boat typically used to ferry people across the river moored near a wooden dock. The man aboard was taking payment from another man on shore.

"That must be them," Robert said, spurring his horse into a gallop and charging toward the boat.

Edna wasn't sure they were going to make it in time and she was right. The boat pushed off from the shore just as they reached it.

"I'll go after the boat. Ye get Allard," Robert shouted to Angus.

Allard was about to mount his horse for a quick getaway, when Angus grabbed him by the back of his cloak and tossed him to the ground.

"Doona move or ye'll regret it," Angus drew his sword to make his point.

Edna turned to see where Robert was. He'd made it to the boat and had climbed aboard. Indiscernible shouting came from the boat and a moment later Robert was seen tossing the boatman overboard.

"Angus!" Edna shouted. "The boatman. Get him before he tries to run."

She took the sword from Angus and held it at Allard's throat. "Doona even think of trying anything. I'm better with a sword than ye may think."

~

Robert heard Angus drag the boatman to shore while he scanned the boat looking for anywhere Emilie might be hidden. It was not a large boat and there were no others aboard that he could see, but he drew his dirk anyway. He'd be prepared if anyone tried to stop him. "Emilie!" he called, but there was no answer. There was no movement either. It seemed it was a one-man crew. He spotted a small wooden cabin towards the back of the boat and headed that way. Opening the door, he found Emilie seated in a corner of the small closet-like room tied and gagged. Relief washed over him as he descended on her, taking her into his arms. "Emilie. Emilie." He kissed her head. "Are ye all right?" He didn't wait for an answer before he began examining her and checking to see if she was hurt.

The muffled sounds of her crying brought his attention to the gag in her mouth. He tore it away and Emilie, with hands still tied in front of her, reached up to hold his face, drawing him close. Robert took a moment to look into her eyes before covering her lips with his own in a kiss that was filled with so many emotions. All would be well. He had her here in his arms once again.

"Did they hurt ye?" Robert asked, knowing that if they did the two men would pay dearly for it.

"I'm fine. I knew you would save me." She gazed adoringly into his eyes.

"I promise I always will." He untied her wrists and helped her stand.

Once they were safely on deck, Robert grabbed the long oar and brought the boat back to the dock, where Angus met them and helped Emilie off the boat.

Robert hopped from the boat and joined them, taking Emilie into his arms and holding her close.

"What about my money?" The boatman asked. He was now soaking wet and down on the ground with Allard.

"Talk to him about it," Angus pointed to Allard who had remained motionless under Edna's glare.

"Emilie, we were so worried for ye. These two had better no' have laid a hand on ye." Edna glared at the two men.

"I didn't touch her. I promise," Allard shouted from his position on the ground. He scrambled to his feet and went for his horse.

Before he could get there, Angus yanked him back down to the ground. With a quick search of Allard's bags, he retrieved some rope to bind both men's hands and feet while Edna held them at sword point. "Ye dinna think we'd let ye get away with what ye've done, did ye?"

"What they've been doing," Edna corrected him.

Robert could tell she wanted to make good use of the sword in her hand but knew there was another way. "We'll take them to the nearest town and leave them with the authorities there," he said.

Edna reluctantly nodded then stepped back from the prisoners and handed the sword back to Angus. Turning to Emilie, she took her into her arms and held her tight. Robert could see the tears on her cheeks, but couldn't bring himself to let go of his Emilie. He had so afraid he would lose her. If he had a choice in the matter, she wouldn't leave his side for a long time.

"Watch it there!" Robert turned in time to see that Angus had hoisted both men across Allard's horse and had them secured so they wouldn't fall. "Do ye need a hand there, Angus?"

"I think I can handle these two. Ye have yer hands full there."

With that, Edna chuckled and let go of Emilie. "I'm so pleased yer safe, lass." With a smile to Robert, she walked away to give them some privacy.

Robert continued holding her close to his chest. "I thought we'd lost ye."

"I'm so happy you didn't." Emilie buried her head in his chest. "We can be together now."

A sense of relief came over all of them.

"Aye, ye can," Edna said. "Now, plans will need to be made to see that ye have a place to go where ye can live yer lives without trouble. I'm no' sure Marie will be happy that ye've escaped, but we'll be sure ye are far enough away that she cannae get to ye."

Edna and Angus mounted their horses. Angus ponied the two men on Allard's horse alongside his own. Emilie rode with Robert, who seemed more than happy to hold onto her forever. Emilie yawned and then a small, relieved smile appeared on her face. "We rode all night to get here. I didn't sleep a wink."

"I believe we all need a good rest before we make our plans," Edna said, feeling the effects of her magic wearing off.

"There is a town nearby. We should be able to find a place to rest and have a good meal there," Robert said.

"We'll celebrate," Edna said. "It does me heart good to see ye two together."

THEY CAME to a small inn on the outskirts of a not-so-small village. Angus got them two rooms upstairs and paid for them. "This purse of yers has come in handy."

"One of me best ideas yet," Edna said. "I doona ken whether I want to eat or sleep first," Edna said, feeling a yawn coming on. She hid it behind her hand as she waited for the others to say something.

"I'm quite hungry," Angus said.

"As am I," Robert added.

"What about ye, Emilie?" Edna asked.

"Food. I haven't eaten since yesterday."

"Food it is then," Edna said.

"Robert and I will drop these two off in the village. We'll be back shortly and then we can eat." They headed off with their two complaining prisoners, leaving Edna and Emilie behind.

"Let's go upstairs and get cleaned up, shall we?" Edna led the way up to their rooms. "I'll see ye shortly." She went into her room and after washing her face and hands, lay down on the bed to wait for the men to return. She might just get a short nap in before they got back.

A small dining area was set up on the first floor. There were three tables, none of which were occupied. The size of the place made it clear that it was a very small business and they were the only customers.

They sat at one of the tables while the person who'd rented them the rooms rushed past them and through a door at the end of the room. He came back a few moments later with a whole roasted chicken, potatoes, carrots and peas. A platter of cheese, butter and bread was also set on the table. It was a humble but lovely spread.

"It's all we have today. Enjoy." He left them with everything they needed and came back moments later with a jug of wine.

"Is it always this quiet?" Edna asked, as he poured each of them a glass.

"Yes, but this is our home. If we have guests, we are happy. If we do not, we are happy." The man smiled and went back to the kitchen leaving them alone.

"We have an inn back home. We doona live there anymore, but me niece and her husband run the place for us." Edna glanced around the room, noticing that it was spotlessly clean. It showed that the owners took great pride in their inn, just as she had with The Thistle & Hive.

"Where do ye live now?" Robert asked.

"Edinburgh," Angus said. He helped himself to a chicken leg. "It's where Edna's work has brought us."

They each helped themselves to the food and when they were done, Edna suggested a walk to help digest their food.

"I never like to lie down right after eating. We can walk a little and talk. I have some things for ye to consider."

Once they were outside, they walked a short distance away from the village before Edna spoke again. "I ken that ye are unsure of what ye will do next and I wanted to give ye an option that ye may no' have thought about. Emilie, yer family home is gone and Robert ye said there is nothing for ye back home in Scotland. What would ye think about traveling to the future with Angus and me? We would bring ye to Glendaloch, where our inn is located. Ye can stay there and take steps toward making a new life for yerselves. What do ye think?"

Robert and Emilie looked at each other. Edna could see this was going to be more of a challenge for Robert than Emilie. His worried glance lit on Angus.

"I think I would like it," Emilie said. "What do you think, Robert?"

"I'm no' sure. I have many questions." His brow furrowed as he rubbed the back of his neck.

"I will answer them all for ye, but first let me tell ye that I have brought many young men and women to the future from a time even before this one. They are all happy and have found fulfilling ways to live their lives."

"Robert, I ken how ye feel," Angus said. "I have no' always lived in the future. I was from a time more than a hundred years before this one. Edna brought me forward. I've had a good life there. A life I've shared with Edna. Doona be afraid."

"What would I do?" Robert asked. "How would I earn me keep?" Robert scrubbed his hands through his hair before glancing at Emilie. She took his hand in hers and he immediately relaxed.

"At first, it would be easiest for ye to stay with Maggie and Dylan.

Me niece and nephew. They could teach ye all about running an inn. Dylan is a chef and a verra good one, so ye would always have plenty of food to eat. Maggie is like me. She keeps track of those who now live in the past and those who live in our time. If there are any problems that arise, she handles them."

"There are shops in town, a good pub and a doctor," Angus added.

"We doona wish to receive charity. We wish to earn our way," Robert said.

"Robert is right," Emilie said. "You are so very kind to help us. We wouldn't wish to take advantage."

"Understood. I want ye to know there is a place there for ye. Ye would be comfortable, and happy, I believe, but it is up to ye. When we go back to the inn, why doona the two of ye take some time to talk and then tomorrow ye can let me ken what ye think." Edna glanced at Angus who was nodding his head in agreement. "We'll also need to find a bridge nearby if possible."

"A bridge?" Robert asked.

"Aye. It is how I time travel," Edna said.

Robert and Emilie exchanged confused looks.

"If ye decide to leave with us, ye'll see what I'm talking about," she assured them.

The young couple seemed content to leave it at that for the time being. So they all headed back to the inn and to their rooms for the night.

"I'm exhausted," Edna said, once they were in their bed.

"As am I. A good night's sleep on a hopefully comfortable bed will do us both good."

"And then tomorrow we go home."

"Once we settle things with Robert and Emilie," Edna clarified. "I doona like the idea of leaving them here without a plan."

"If they decide no' to come with us, then we'll stay here for a while longer to make sure they get settled."

"Fingers crossed they want to travel with us to Glendaloch." Edna could see that Angus was more than ready to go home.

～

"WHAT DO YOU THINK?" Emilie asked. She sat on a small wooden stool by the hearth as Robert made a fire to keep them warm.

"I'm no' sure. Are ye no' afraid to go?" he asked.

She wrinkled her brow and tipped her head to the side, gazing into the fire as she thought. "I'm not. Are you surprised?"

"Perhaps a little," Robert said. "It is the unknown that we'd be heading into."

"At this moment our future is unknown no matter what we choose. There are no guarantees we will find a place here in France or in Scotland. I have no family and yours, from what you've told me, might not be willing to help you."

"I doona believe they will," Robert said. It was clear to Robert that she knew what she wanted to do, but he had so many questions. If the frown he was wearing was any indication of his feelings, then they might be staying.

"Why do you frown so, Robert? Do you not wish to go?" Emilie reached out to touch his arm. "Edna and Angus want to help us. They are good people. I trust them. Do you?"

"I do. They have helped us to this point." He knelt in front of Emilie, taking her hands in his. When he looked at Emilie he had a picture in his mind of what their life together would be. He had no idea what to expect in the future or how he would even be able to take care of her and any bairns they'd have. "What do ye think it will be like there?"

"I think it will be so much more wonderful than the world we know. Angus told me that it takes little time to travel almost anywhere."

"How is that possible?" Robert asked.

"I don't know, but I think I'd like to find out," Emilie said.

Robert looked down at his hands. He was having a hard time with the idea of leaving what was familiar to them. Giving up control of their lives to a future they knew nothing about gave him pause.

Emilie touched his cheek with her hand, and he lifted his head to gaze at her. "We'd have each other. What more do we need?"

He released a sigh. "Yer right, but I'd like more time to think."

"We should give them our decision tomorrow morning. I feel sure they want to go back home."

"I imagine they do. Shall we get some sleep?" Robert asked.

Emilie yawned in answer.

"There is only one bed. I will sleep on the floor." Robert was about to retrieve his extra plaid to use for a blanket when Emilie's hand on his arm froze him in place.

"You can sleep with me. I don't mind." Emilie blushed as she looked away.

It took a moment for Robert to speak and when he did the words came out with a stammer. "But we arenae married."

"We will be." Emilie undressed down to her shift and climbed into bed.

"Are ye sure?" Robert asked. "I willnae be able to keep my hands off of ye."

"Robert, I love you. I know we will be by each other's side forever, no matter what lies ahead."

Robert hesitated, fighting with the desire of his heart and his honor as a gentleman.

Emilie nodded her head and smiled letting him know it was all right. She watched as Robert took off his kilt but kept his long shirt on. He carefully laid the kilt on the bench, lining his boots up side by side as he had done in the barracks of the palace. When he turned to face her, she was smiling at him. He was drawn to her, with careful movements, he climbed into the bed and pulled the blankets over them.

Emilie rolled onto her side, placing her head on his chest and her hand on his belly. They'd done this many times in the garden, although they'd been fully clothed each and every time. Robert cradled her in his arms while she moved closer. They had never done more than kissing and touching and he was determined to honor her, leaving any other desires aside until they were married. No matter how difficult that might be.

Emilie propped herself up on her elbow so she could look into Robert's eyes. He was captivated by her, as always, but now he knew that he would have the pleasure of gazing at her every day for the rest of his life.

She leaned over and kissed his lips, and just like in the garden he wanted to touch every inch of her soft skin. This time there was nothing keeping them from going further than they had in the past. There was no danger of prying eyes. But he wouldn't push her. She gently touched his lips again with her own, while brushing her hand through his hair.

Robert held very still to fight the needs she was kindling in him.

Then Emilie's hand traveled even lower than his belly. In one swift move, Robert rolled atop her. "Are ye sure this is what ye want?" he asked, his breathing ragged and his heart pounding.

She looked at him with determination, a fire in her eyes he had never seen before. "More than anything," she replied.

"If ye tell me to stop, I will." He reassured her before kissing her neck in the tender spot he knew would arouse her even more than she already was.

"Don't stop. Don't ever stop." He decided then and there that he would make all of her wishes come true.

# SEVENTEEN

At breakfast the next morning, Edna couldn't help but notice the change in both Robert and Emilie. She couldn't hide her smile but decided not to comment on theirs. "Well, what is yer decision?"

Robert glanced at Emilie before he spoke. "We've decided we'll go with ye."

Edna clapped her hands together and nearly jumped out of her seat. "Oh, I'm so excited. It will be wonderful, ye'll see."

"We ken it will. We're a bit nervous, but ye'll be there to help us," Robert said.

"We'll finish our breakfast and then all we need is a bridge." Edna reached across the table to squeeze their hands.

The innkeeper arrived carrying a large platter. "Good morning. I hope you slept well."

"We did," Angus said. "What have we here?"

"I've brought some eggs, fresh this morning from our hens. Bread, cheese and some ham." He placed the platter in the middle of the table so that they could help themselves.

"It looks wonderful," Emilie said as she helped herself to some eggs.

"Sir, is there a bridge anywhere nearby?" Angus asked as the innkeeper began to walk away.

He turned back to the table, seeming puzzled that they would ask about something like that. "If you continue through the village, on this same road you will come to one that crosses over a small stream. It is a bit of a distance. You cannot miss it."

"Thank ye for yer help. Ye have a lovely inn here, we've enjoyed our stay," Angus said.

"Perhaps we will see you again," the innkeeper bowed his head and left them.

Edna and Angus ate heartily, but Emilie and Robert only picked at their food.

"Is everything all right?" Edna asked.

"I thought I was hungry at first, but then my appetite left me," Emilie said.

"Are ye nervous?" Angus asked.

"I think that must be it," she replied.

"I feel much the same," Robert said.

"It's understandable. This will be a big change for both of ye. All I can say is that I'm sure ye'll think it's worth it but if once we get there ye find ye are not happy, we can send ye back."

That seemed to give them some reassurance, though they were still uninterested in eating.

After breakfast, they took their time gathering their things and then rode their horses in the direction the innkeeper had sent them. It was further than they'd anticipated, but it was a beautiful day and they enjoyed the scenery along the way.

"I feel bad that we've taken Louis' horses," Angus said. "But I doona believe there's any way to get them back to him without riding to Tuileries, and we're no' going anywhere near there."

"He'll be fine about it. He probably willnae miss them at all," Robert assured Angus. "Will we take them with us through time?"

"We've traveled with horses before. They'll be fine," Edna said.

They reached the bridge at around noontime and once everyone was settled, Edna began the process of transporting them all to the future. Robert and Emilie were understandably nervous, but Edna did her best to keep them calm with her instructions. They all stayed atop their horses and banded very close together.

"Robert hold onto Emilie. Emilie take me hand and I'll take yers Angus. Are we all ready?"

Everyone acknowledged that they were and before long the swirling fog, dotted with flashing bits of colorful lights engulfed them. When it stopped they were on the bridge in Glendaloch.

"We've arrived," Edna announced. Two young lads throwing rocks into the stream looked up in surprise. When they saw that it was Edna and Angus they waved and went back to tossing stones.

"It's good to be home," Angus said, breathing deeply and filling his lungs with the familiar scent of Glendaloch.

"This is the future?" Robert asked. "It looks nae different."

"I ken the bridge and the surrounding area doesnae look much different from yer time but wait until we get to town. I think ye're going to love it. Ye might feel overwhelmed at first, but please ken that we are all here for ye and we want ye to feel as comfortable as possible."

"It's exciting," Emilie said. She hadn't stopped smiling since breakfast that morning.

"Let's go," Angus said. He led the way along the path that would take them to The Thistle & Hive Inn.

Robert held Emilie close the whole time. They were so busy gazing at each other that they weren't aware of the fact that they were now approaching the main road that ran through Glendaloch.

"This is it." Edna glanced at the two of them.

They finally broke their gaze and looked around. Wonder and awe spread from one to the other as they saw for the first time where and when they would be living. Cars whizzed by as they approached the road and the horses danced in place as they were spooked by the strange sights and sounds.

"What was that?" Robert asked, calming his horse.

"That is a car. It is one of the ways we travel in this time," Angus said.

"I can see why it doesn't take very long to get anywhere," Emilie said.

"The inn is just ahead. These are some of the shops we told ye about. We've got a bookshop and a pharmacy. There's the pub. Dr. Ferguson's office is down the road a bit, but he's no' always there." Edna pointed out each of the places she was talking about. "There is also a stable," Edna looked back over her shoulder to the direction the stable was in. "So, if ye wish to ride there are horses available to ye. Angus keeps his horse there."

"I'd like to visit as long as we're here," Angus said.

"Look Angus, it's Teddy!" She waved at a young man who was waving at them and running their way.

"Edna! Ye're back," Teddy said.

"We are. How are ye, Teddy?"

"Well. Would ye like me to take yer horses?" he asked.

"Werenae we lucky ye were right close by," Edna said. She dismounted and handed the reins to Teddy.

As the others dismounted, Teddy took their horses as well.

"Teddy, this is Robert MacMillan and Emilie Toussaint. They'll be living here at the inn," Edna explained.

"A pleasure to meet ye," Teddy said.

"Tell Mrs. McDougall I'll be by to see me horse soon and let her ken that Robert here will likely want to come by to ride."

"I'll be sure to tell Mrs. McDougall."

"I'd like that," Robert said.

Once Teddy was headed off, Angus opened the door to the inn and ushered them inside.

"Maggie!" Edna called.

A very pregnant Maggie waddled out of the office. It took a moment for it to register what she was seeing. Once she did, she ran toward Edna and Angus, who engulfed her in a hug.

"Please doona run, dear," Edna said.

"Ye're here!" Maggie shouted.

"I told ye we'd arrive as soon as we could. We wanted to be here for ye and Dylan when the babies arrived."

"Ye're just in time. Any day now," she said, glancing at Robert and Emilie.

"We're also here because we thought ye might need some help. Robert and Emilie are new arrivals from the seventeenth century."

"I gathered as much. Emilie's dress gave her away." Maggie smiled warmly at the couple. "Welcome. We're happy to have ye here with us. I'm Maggie."

"Robert MacMillan and Emilie Toussaint," Robert said.

"I thought that while they get their bearings, they could do some of the things ye and Dylan normally do. That way ye can enjoy the babies."

"That would be amazing," Maggie said. "Dylan! He should be in the kitchen."

"I'm right here," Dylan said, emerging from the dining room.

"Edna! Angus! This is a pleasant surprise." Dylan hugged each of them.

"They've brought some guests with them. This is Robert MacMillan and Emilie Toussaint. They're here from the seventeenth century."

"They are officially time travelers," Edna said.

"It's a pleasure to meet you," Dylan said. "Are you hungry? I'm making some barbecue ribs on the grill out back, corn on the cob and potato salad. All of Maggie's favorites."

"I think they might be yer favorites," Maggie teased. "These babies are taking up so much room that I cannae eat a big meal these days."

"I'm sure Emilie and Robert must be getting hungry. They hardly touched their breakfast this morning," Edna said.

"Ye must have been nervous," Maggie said. "I cannae say I blame ye."

"Well, it will be a little while longer. Why don't you show them around town and by the time you're back everything will be ready?"

"It's good to be back," Angus said, as they left the inn and headed down the street.

"Are ye having regrets about the move to Edinburgh?" Edna was concerned. She thought he liked their new life.

"Of course no'. Can I no' miss this as well?" Angus said.

"I just want to be sure yer happy."

"As I've told ye, as long as I'm with ye I would be happy anywhere."

Robert and Emilie's heads hadn't stopped moving from side-to-side and up and down. They were taking in all of the unusual things they'd never seen before.

"I cannae believe me eyes," Robert said.

"Ye'll get used to it all," Edna said. "As I mentioned, I've brought several people back to this time from the sixteenth century. They've become quite adept at living in this time. As a matter of fact, I've been told by many they would never want to go back."

"I don't believe you've told us what year it is," Emilie said.

"It's the year 2022," Edna replied.

Emilie shook her head in disbelief.

They wandered up and down the main road. Edna introduced them to anyone they met along the way. Robert and Emilie were assured by all that they were most welcome in Glendaloch and were told if they ever needed anything all they had to do was ask.

"Everyone is so kind," Robert said. "I think we will be happy here."

"I believe we will," Emilie said, smiling sweetly up at him.

"We should head back now," Angus said. "I believe Dylan will be ready for us and I for one am hungry again."

~

MAGGIE AND DYLAN were waiting to greet them when they got back. "We'll have to get ye both settled in. Emilie, I've got some clothing ye can borrow until we get ye things of yer own," Maggie said, rubbing her belly. "None of it fits me right now."

"Thank you," Emilie said. "My dress is out of place, although most of the people we met didn't even seem to notice."

"They're used to seeing people from different times roaming around town," Angus informed her.

"Come on into the dining room and have a seat. I'll get the food and drinks." Dylan hurried back through the kitchen door.

Edna and Angus led their guests to the family table where they'd always sat for their meals.

Dylan returned with a tray of food which he placed on the table in front of them. "Dig in."

"It smells delicious," Robert said, eyeing the ribs.

"Help yourselves," Dylan said. "Ale?"

"Aye," Robert and Angus both said at once.

"Ice water for Maggie," he said, gazing at his wife.

"Ice water?" Emilie asked.

"Ice water is water with ice cubes in it. We have something called a freezer and it makes little cubes of ice to put in yer drink. It makes it nice and cold," Edna said. "Ye'll have so many new things to learn about."

"I'll get some for you, Emilie, so you can try it. Edna?" Dylan was at the bar now, gathering their drinks on a tray.

"Please," Edna replied.

"This is a nice surprise," Maggie said, passing the potato salad to Emilie. "It's wonderful to have a family meal together again."

Dylan placed all the drinks on the table and then held his glass up. "Welcome home to those who've lived here before and to those who are new to Glendaloch."

The meal was a success. The newcomers enjoyed everything very much and complimented Dylan on his cooking skills.

"I'll be sure to teach you all of my tricks," Dylan said. "Once the twins arrive, I'll need help in the kitchen."

"And I'll need help with the guests," Maggie said.

"I'm sure they're up for the task," Edna said.

Robert took hold of Emilie's hand. "We are happy to be of service, but first, I wonder if there would be a place for us to marry." He kissed Emilie's hand.

"Aye. There's a small chapel here in town," Maggie said.

"I'll make the arrangements for ye," Edna said. Her first job as a member of the Council of Witches had been a success and she couldn't be happier. She hoped they wouldn't be upset that she'd brought Emilie and Robert to the future. It really was the only option that made sense.

"Are you a witch, as well, Maggie?" Emilie asked.

"Aye, although I've been so preoccupied with the twins' birth that I havenae used me skills much."

"Have ye heard anything from the Mackenzies?" Edna wondered.

"They are all doing well. The children are growing, and it looks like Jenna may be pregnant again."

"Wonderful. Have ye heard from anyone else?"

"No' recently, which tells me all is well with our time traveling family."

"Is Dr. Ferguson in town?" Edna hoped he was. They relied on him for baby deliveries in both the past and present.

"He is. He got back last week and brought Lady Catherine with him. They'll be staying in town for a while, so he'll definitely be here for the arrival of the twins."

"That's a relief," Edna said.

"I wasnae worried. He's always verra good about being wherever and whenever it is he needs to be." Maggie pushed herself up out of the chair and started to clear the plates which made everyone else jump up too.

"Dylan, why doona ye show Robert and Emilie around. I'm going to call down to Pastor Robins to arrange for a wedding and Angus can clear the table. Maggie, ye should go sit down."

"All right," Dylan said. "You've seen the lobby and the dining room. I'll show you the kitchen, the garden and the cottage where Maggie and I live." He led them through the doors into the kitchen.

Edna left Angus in the dining room while she went into her old office to call down to Pastor Robins. He answered right away.

"Hello, Pastor Robins, this is Edna Campbell."

"Edna, how are ye? Are ye back in town?" he asked.

"I'm here until after the babies are born."

"We've missed ye and Angus."

"We've missed all of ye as well. I was wondering how quickly we could arrange a wedding at the chapel."

"How soon did ye want it?" he asked.

"Would now be too soon?" she asked.

"What's the rush?"

"Nae rush at all. It's just that this couple has been waiting for some time to wed and they've traveled a good distance to get here."

"Is this one of yer time traveling couples, Edna?" the pastor asked.

He'd been skeptical the first time he'd met one of Edna's people, but had come to realize that it was all true. People were traveling back and forth through time right here in Glendaloch and who was he to question it.

"They are a sweet couple. I'll let them give ye all the details, but they just want to be married as soon as possible."

"Give me about an hour. It's just a small group, aye?"

"Just us," Edna said.

"All right. I'll see ye soon then."

Edna hung up and went to find Maggie. She found them all out back in the garden.

"This is beautiful," Emilie said when she saw Edna.

"I'm glad ye like it. It's no' the gardens at Tuileries, but I think it's perfect."

"Dylan showed us their cottage and was going to take us upstairs to our room," Robert said.

That thought made Edna pause, the guest rooms are lovely but they aren't really set up for someone to live in long term. So she quickly made a decision. "Maggie, I think they should take our rooms on the first floor."

"Are you sure? I thought you might want to use them," Dylan said.

"We're just here visiting. Emilie and Robert will be living here. They'll need the extra space to be comfortable." Edna was having some mixed feelings about giving up their rooms, but she and Angus had already decided their life would be in Edinburg for the foreseeable future. It was only right to make Emilie and Robert as comfortable as possible. There would always be a room available for Edna and Angus when they visited.

"Perfect. We'll have to get it ready for them," he said.

"I'll help. But before we do that, Pastor Robins said we can go down to the chapel and he'll marry ye right away." Edna checked the time. "We'll be a little early, but he willnae mind."

Emilie clapped her hands in excitement as Robert swept her off the ground and spun her around.

Edna and Maggie couldn't stop smiling as they watched the happy couple.

"This is why we do what we do," Edna said.

"I hope ye doona mind if I doona go with ye. I'm feeling a little tired and I think I'd like to lie down for a while."

"That's fine, dear. Ye rest. Angus and I will escort them and be their witnesses, but first I want to pick some flowers for Emilie's bouquet."

She retrieved her old pruning shears from the potting table and went to work. Maggie followed along beside her, pointing out the flowers she thought were the prettiest. Roses, daisies, lavender and baby's breath made a colorful and fragrant nosegay.

"I'll get some ribbon to tie it," Maggie said as she slowly made her way back to the cottage.

Edna pruned off all the thorns and arranged them in her hand. Maggie returned with a wide pink ribbon which she wrapped around the flowers and then tied into a bow.

The women held them out at arm's length to look over their work.

"Perfect," Maggie said.

Edna motioned for Robert and Emilie to join her. "Pastor Robins is waiting for us, so we should go."

They collected Angus on their way out the door. Robert and Emilie held hands as they walked, asking questions about this and that and pretty much everything they'd never seen before.

Edna was so happy for them. They would have a good life together and she was happy to be a small part of it.

Pastor Robins made the ceremony brief yet meaningful. He'd lit candles all around the small chapel and the twinkling of the flames gave the quiet sanctuary a romantic glow. It was clear that it would be a cherished memory. Robert surprised them all by presenting Emilie with a wedding ring he removed from his sporran.

"I've been holding onto it for some time now. I thought I would never get to give it to ye, but I'm so happy to do so now."

"It's beautiful," Emilie said, admiring it on her finger. "And it fits."

"It belonged to me mother. She gave it to me and said it should be for me wife."

"That makes it all the more special," Edna said. She wiped a tear from her eyes with a hankie Angus handed her.

"I came prepared," he said with a small chuckle. "Ye always cry at weddings."

"I cannae help it. Weddings are the promise of a future for every couple. What they do with it, well that's up to them. There's something about the commitment that they are making to each other that gets to me every time."

"It does me, too," Angus said with a sniffle.

"Do ye need my hankie?" Edna teased.

"I've me own." He pulled another hankie from his sporran and dabbed at his own teary eyes.

When the ceremony was over they headed back to the inn to celebrate.

While everyone was busy in the dining room, Edna went into the suite she and Angus had shared. Everything was neat and clean, but it wasn't theirs. They had moved everything to their new home and it was time for someone else to build a life here. She got fresh sheets and blankets from the linen closet and while she placed them on the bed, she became a little melancholy as she thought about her life here in Glendaloch.

"Edna, what are ye thinking?" she said to herself. "Yer doing just what ye always wanted to do."

"Talking to yerself?" Angus asked from the doorway.

"Aye."

"Let me help ye." He tucked the blanket in and then topped it with a quilt before turning to Edna. "It's strange being back."

"That it is. I was just reliving old memories."

"We've new ones to make, but this place will always be here so that when we're tired of making new memories we can come home."

"Have I told ye that I love ye yet today?" Edna asked.

"Ye havenae and I've been waiting to hear it," Angus teased.

"I love ye," Edna uttered those three simple words as often as she could.

"I love ye," Angus answered, kissing her sweetly and then hugging her close to his heart.

CHAPTER

# EIGHTEEN

Edna had just closed her eyes when there was a loud knocking on the door.

"Edna, the babies are coming," Dylan sounded frantic on the other side of the door.

"We'll be right there," she said, nudging Angus and then hopping out of bed. "Have ye called Dr. Ferguson?"

"He'll meet us at the hospital. I'm going to go help Maggie. We'll see you in the lobby."

"The babies are coming, Angus, we must hurry." She changed her clothes as quickly as she could. Angus did the same and then they ran downstairs.

Emilie and Robert were standing with Maggie and Dylan. Emilie looked like a deer in the headlights as her eyes darted back and forth between Maggie and Robert. "Will she be...?"

"She'll be fine, dear. Doona worry. Ye and Robert stay here."

"There are no guests here now and none expected, so you don't have to worry about any of that. The kitchen is stocked with food in case we aren't back in the morning." Dylan was rattling off anything he could think of.

"Ye're doing surprisingly well," Angus said to Dylan.

"I've been planning this out in my head for months now. I'm going to get the car. Are you okay, Maggie?"

"I'm fine," she said, not sounding fine at all.

Dylan hurried out back to get the car. Edna held Maggie's hand. "Remember to breathe. All will be well and before ye ken it there will be two wee ones for us all to love."

"The car's here," Angus said, holding the inn door open for Maggie and Edna. "We'll be back."

"Good luck to ye all," Robert said as they hurried to the car.

The hospital wasn't far, but Dylan made it in record time and for that, Edna was grateful. "Yer an excellent driver, Dylan."

"Thanks. Anything to take my mind off the pain Maggie is in."

"I'm okay right now."

Dylan ran inside the hospital and before long a nurse with a wheelchair met them and wheeled her inside.

"Dr. Ferguson," Edna said, as he rushed into view. "'Tis good to see ye."

"Good to see ye back in town. We'll chat more later. For now, I've got some babies to deliver. Come along, Dylan."

Edna grabbed onto Angus' hand as she watched Maggie being wheeled away. "I guess there's naething for us to do but wait."

"Come sit," Angus said, leading her to a small room equipped with comfy chairs and a television. "We might be here a while."

"I'm so nervous," Edna said. "I hope it all goes well."

"Dr. Ferguson will see to it," Angus assured her.

Edna sat in a comfy recliner facing the door and Angus sat right next to her and held her hand.

"We may as well relax. They'll come find us when there's news," Angus said.

He reclined his chair and closed his eyes. Edna glanced over at him and wished she could be as relaxed as he was right now. She repeated a spell over and over in her head. It was one she used whenever she needed to be calmed, and before long, it worked. Then she, too, reclined her chair and was able to close her eyes and fall asleep.

~

"Edna," Dr. Ferguson's voice was soft and seemed very far away. "The babies have arrived."

Edna's eyes shot open and she sat straight up. "What? The babies?"

"Aye. Maggie is doing well and so are the twins. She's had a boy and a girl."

"Oh, my! Angus wake up! The babies are here."

Angus opened his eyes and stretched his arms overhead.

"They've had a boy and a girl." It was a surprise to both Edna and Angus. Maggie wanted to keep it a secret and had done a very good job of it.

"Oh that's wonderful! Can we see them?"

"Aye. Right this way."

Edna and Angus followed Dr. Ferguson down the hallway, past the nurse's station.

"Congratulations," the nurses said as they passed.

"Here they are," Dr. Ferguson said, stopping in front of a doorway and ushering them in. "I'll be back in a while."

"Oh, my!" Edna gushed on seeing the babies in the arms of their mother and father. "They're beautiful!"

"This is Maura," Maggie said.

"This is Declan," Dylan said.

"Would ye like to hold them?" Maggie asked.

Edna held out her arms and took wee Maura in them. She wondered if the little lass would have the same gift that she and Maggie had. It would be wonderful to have another witch in the family. Either way, these babies would be loved so very much. Edna placed her finger in Maura's wee hand. Her slender, tiny fingers wrapped around it and squeezed. Edna's eyes popped open in surprise. "She's a strong one!"

Angus held little Declan, staring adoringly down at his wee face. Declan had chubby little cheeks and a sprig of dark hair. He stared up at Angus seeming to know that this was the man who would spoil him every chance he got.

"I should call yer mother and father," Edna said.

"It's already done," Dylan replied. "They are on vacation in Spain, but they'll leave as soon as they can get a flight home. They can't wait to meet their little grandbabies."

"Can ye believe it, Auntie?" Maggie said. "They're here."

"Aye, they are and they're so verra beautiful, just like ye."

Dylan cleared his throat, making Edna laugh. "And ye," she assured him.

"Thank you for noticing," Dylan teased.

They handed the babies back to their parents. Outside the windows, the sun was rising. "When will ye be able to come home?"

"Dr. Ferguson thought I should stay one more night. So tomorrow morning."

"Ye must be exhausted," Edna said.

"Surprisingly no'," Maggie said. "I feel refreshed for some strange reason."

They stayed a while and gushed over the babies and Maggie. Edna didn't really want to leave, but she wanted Maggie and Dylan to have some time alone with Maura and Declan.

"We should be going," she said.

Dylan handed Angus the car keys. "You can take the car. I'm going to stay here with my wife and my babies." His smile couldn't be any bigger. "I'm a dad!"

"We'll head back to the inn. Call us when yer ready to come home and I'll come get ye," Angus said.

"We will," Dylan said, walking with them to the door. "Thank you, Edna. None of this would have been possible without you."

"I'm happy to see that me meddling has resulted in the creation of a happy little family."

He kissed her on the cheek and gave Angus a hug. Edna was overcome with emotion. "So much love. So much happiness."

Angus wrapped an arm around her shoulders and walked her to the car. They stood in the parking lot for a while as he held Edna in his arms and the sun made its way higher in the sky.

THE NEXT SEVERAL days at the inn were a whirlwind. Edna and Emilie did all they could to be of assistance to Maggie. They changed diapers whenever necessary and held the babies as often as possible.

"Emilie, ye are going to be a good mother someday," Edna said.

"Do you really believe so?" Emilie asked.

"I do. Ye really have a way with Maura and Declan."

Edna was impressed with Emilie's maternal instincts and her willingness to do anything that Maggie needed, especially since she'd wondered if Emilie would be up to the task. Her entire life had been spent being cared for and catered to by servants, and she'd never really had a chance to do this kind of thing. Edna felt good that when she and Angus left for Edinburgh, Maggie and Dylan would have all the help they needed, especially since Maggie's mother and father had arrived the day before.

Robert spent a good deal of time following Dylan around and learning the ropes of being a chef and running an inn. He was worried at first that he wouldn't be able to do it, but Dylan assured him that he wasn't going anywhere and he'd be right there if Robert needed any help with anything. Although, like Emilie, he was fitting in well and was a fast learner. Edna had no worries at all that they would succeed and thrive in their new lives.

"We've been so lucky to have had ye and Uncle Angus here with us. I cannae thank ye enough for bringing Emilie and Robert to us.

They've been a great help. Once they get the hang of everything around here, we'll have a lot more free time on our hands.

"As much as I hate to leave ye, yer Uncle Angus and I must get back to Edinburgh. William will be peeved we've been away so long and I must report in to the council." Edna wiped away a tear that was followed by another and another. "Oh..."

Maggie's voice broke as she spoke "We understand. It's been so nice having ye here with us. When will ye come for another visit?" She handed Edna a tissue and grabbed one to blot at her own teary eyes.

"It will be hard to keep us away. Those sweet little bairns will be growing so fast. We'll want to spend as much time with them as we can."

"Good. That's what I was hoping ye'd say."

"I'm going to go find yer uncle. We'll be back to see ye before we leave."

EDNA FOUND Angus in his favorite spot reading his newspaper. "Me love, I believe it's time we headed back to Edinburgh."

"I was thinking the same," Angus answered. He folded the newspaper and set it on the side table next to the chair.

"Dylan will drive us to the train station," Edna said. "Ye're sure ye're ready?"

"I am, but are ye?" Angus tipped his head, eyeing her with a cocked brow.

"Of course I am. I must report in at the council. I called to tell them I'd be back in the office tomorrow, so they'll be expecting me." She glanced around the lobby of the inn experiencing an unmistakable tug on her heartstrings. "We'll be back for a visit before ye ken it," she said as much for herself as for Angus.

"Let's say our goodbyes to Emilie and Robert," Angus said.

"Where are they?" Edna asked.

"Robert's in the kitchen," Angus said, heading in that direction.

They found him busy chopping vegetables and tossing them into a pot. Dylan was doing the same.

"We're going to be on our way," Edna said on seeing them. "We wanted to come say goodbye to Robert and Emilie."

"I'll go get the car." Dylan washed his hands and then headed outside.

"Emilie's out in the garden," Robert said. He put down his knife and wiped his hands on his apron. Edna and Angus followed him as he led the way out the back door.

Out in the garden, Emilie was picking some fresh herbs. "Emilie, Edna and Angus will be going home," Robert said.

She put the herbs in her basket. "We'll be sorry to see you go."

"Come here, me dear." Edna held out her arms and Emilie rushed into them for a hug. "Ye are going to be the best thing that has happened to Glendaloch in a long time. I'm going to miss ye, but I ken ye will be just fine without me."

Robert and Angus shook hands and hugged, before Robert joined Emilie and hugged Edna. "Robert, ye give the best hugs."

Edna gazed at Angus. "Doona worry, yers are even better."

Angus chuckled as did Robert and Emilie.

"Thank ye for all ye've done for us," Robert said. "We are truly happy to be here and looking forward to what life in Glendaloch will bring us."

"We love you both so very much and will forever be indebted to you." Emilie got a little teary-eyed, which set Edna off as well.

Angus handed her a hankie and she used it to dry her eyes before hugging Emilie one more time.

"We'll be back. Ye havenae seen the last of us," Angus said. "Those bairns are quite the draw."

Maggie opened the door of the cottage. "I hear a lot of goodbyes out here." She was holding both babies. Emilie went to her and took Declan. "Now that I've got a free arm, I need a hug."

Edna and Angus obliged, each taking a turn to hug Maggie and tell her and the babies how much they were loved.

"We'll be back in the blink of an eye." Edna wiped away more tears before taking the arm Angus offered her and leaving Glendaloch behind—for now.

~

WILLIAM SAT in the window of their flat eyeing them with kitty disdain. Angus opened the door and Edna hurried in, happy to see William and wanting to pick him up and shower him with love.

William on the other hand let her know exactly what he thought of that. He hopped down from the window and with his tail straight up in the air, walked out of the room without even a rub on her legs.

"I think he's upset," Edna said.

"What gave ye that idea?" Angus chuckled. "It's good to be home. I cannae wait to sleep in me own bed tonight."

"I'm going to get cleaned up and changed and then I'll head to the office to tell the council about our trip."

"I'll see if I can talk some sense into William," Angus said. "It looks like our lovely neighbor brought us some groceries."

"How sweet of her," Edna said. "We'll have to invite her over for dinner."

"No' tonight."

"Nae, of course no'. Tomorrow night would be better if she can make it."

Edna bustled about the flat. She tried talking to William, but he wasn't budging. He'd come around. There was nothing unusual about his behavior. She put on some clean clothes, brushed and fixed her hair, replacing the blue streak which was her signature look and headed off to The Council of Witches.

"You've been gone quite some time," Melusina said when she entered the office.

"Hello to ye, too," Edna said feeling a bit peevish at the greeting she'd received.

"Welcome back," Daire said, motioning her to come sit by her desk.

"Where's Mardella?" Edna asked.

"She's handling some problems in London. She'll be back once she's done," Melusina said, pulling up a chair next to Edna.

"So, tell us all about yer mission," Daire said.

"There's a lot to tell, but the first thing I need to say is that from now on I'll facilitate me own time travel."

Melusina was taken aback, "Why? Was there a problem?"

"Ye sent me back to the right time, but we ended up in this verra close. Angus and I had to find a way to get to Paris that wasnae going to take a month or longer."

Melusina exchanged a look with Daire. "Good to ken. From now on, time travel will be left up to ye."

"Thank ye for understanding. Emilie Toussaint and Robert MacMillan are now married and since it dinna seem practical for them to stay in their own time, they traveled back to Glendaloch with us. They will stay at me inn with me niece and her husband."

"I dinna ken that was part of the plan. I thought ye were just going to help Emilie make her wish come true."

"I did. It wasnae easy and it took some time, but I did what I set out to do."

"I'm sure there's more to the story than that." Daire tapped a pencil on the pad of paper she had in front of her.

"I'll spare you all the details, but Marie de Medici almost made my task impossible. Her son Louis, on the other hand, helped a great deal."

"Ye met Louis XIII?" Melusina seemed impressed.

"We did."

"And ye feel that all worked out as it should?"

"In the end. Robert and Emilie were meant to be together. It was obvious from the verra beginning. Love is a journey. Theirs started out with less-than-ideal circumstances, but they are now verra happy. They married in Glendaloch and me niece will take care of any needs they may have, even if it means they wish to return to their own time."

"It sounds like ye worked everything out satisfactorily."

"I believe I did."

"We're happy to hear it because once ye have had a chance to rest, we have something new for ye to sink yer teeth into."

Edna was relieved they were pleased with the outcome of her mission and happy there was at least one more to come.

"Go home to yer husband and William. Enjoy a few days off and then we'll discuss yer next assignment."

Edna wouldn't ask what that next assignment would be. If they told her, she'd probably want to leave immediately to go wherever and whenever they needed her.

# EPILOGUE

"We should call Maggie and see if they need us to pick anything up while we're out," Robert said.

Emilie removed her phone from her purse and dialed Maggie. A slight giggle escaped her lips. She pointed at the phone as she held it to her ear. This little thing she held in her hand was one of the most amazing discoveries they'd made about this time. Maggie insisted that they each get one, and at first Emilie was puzzled as to why they might need it, but now she always kept it close at hand. The ringing sound ended abruptly.

"Hi, Emilie," Maggie said when she answered.

"Do you need anything before we head back to the inn?" Emilie asked.

"No' that I can think of. Maura and Declan are napping, so I'm just enjoying some quiet time before they wake up. Ye two take yer time. Have some fun."

"We will. See you when we get back." She placed the phone back in her purse. "They don't need anything and it seems they don't need us," Emilie smiled.

"What shall we do?" Robert asked.

"We've been shopping and we've walked around the village, so maybe we should go to the pub across the street." Emilie had taken to life in Glendaloch and particularly enjoyed the lively atmosphere to be found at the local pub.

"I like that idea."

They took a seat at a booth along the wall. Some local musicians were warming up. Robert and Emilie waved hello to their new friends and neighbors who were already seated at the bar and nearby tables.

"Robert and Emilie! Good to see ye again," Daniel Calhoun, the pub owner said as he approached. "How are ye both today?"

"Verra well, thank ye."

"Ale for ye Robert?" he asked.

"Aye."

"Emilie?"

"Cider, please."

"Coming right up."

"I love it here," Emilie said.

"As do I. I'm so glad we took the chance."

The band started playing a traditional Scottish reel and Emilie found herself tapping her foot to the music.

"Would ye like to dance?" Robert asked, holding out a hand to her.

"I believe I would." Emilie took his hand. They moved closer to the musicians and whirled around the floor. Emilie laughed as Robert spun her around and around. Soon another couple joined them and before long the floor was crowded with people enjoying the music right along with them. Some of the people they'd met and some were new to them, but all were smiling, laughing and enjoying themselves.

Daniel caught Robert's eye and held up their drinks before placing them on the table of their booth.

"Our drinks are ready for us," he said.

They arrived back at their booth out of breath, but still moving to the music.

"This is something I never would have enjoyed at Tuileries," Emilie said. "It was not a happy place for me. I didn't realize it at the time. I thought I was happy at court, or at least content, but not being allowed to make my own decisions and constantly wondering what kind of mood the Queen Mother would be in left me feeling on edge and unfulfilled. I always knew there was more to life and now that I've found it, I can't imagine how I ever thought life at court was good for me." She sipped her cider.

Robert took a swig of his ale. He held his mug in both of his hands as he glanced across the table at Emilie. "It does me heart good to see ye like this."

"Mine too," Emilie said, reaching across the table to hold his hand. "I never dreamed that my life would turn out like this. I had little hope of anything good ever happening for me."

"I felt the same. I ken there had to be something more to life than waiting on the whims of a young king. Doona get me wrong, I enjoyed me time with him, but it was no' as fulfilling as me life here with ye."

"I don't ever want to go back," Emilie said. "There is so much to learn about this time. Perhaps someday we can travel across the ocean and visit lands far away."

"Do ye think ye'd get into one of those, what are they called?" Robert asked.

"Planes," Emilie said.

"Do ye think ye'd want to go that far up in the sky?"

"I do. It must be safe. People do it all the time."

"I wouldnae have thought it, but ye're more adventurous than I."

Robert's position as a soldier and guard in the court of Louis XIII had made him cautious. His nature was to protect Emilie and she understood that anything he saw as a possible threat to her safety was something that required his thoughtful consideration before he would go along with it.

"I'm only brave because you are with me," Emilie said. "When we're together I feel that anything is possible."

"Then we'll do it. Maggie will help us when the time is right."

"Aye. We should probably learn everything we can about the time we're living in before we wander off on our own."

"We'll always come back to Glendaloch though."

"I couldn't imagine living anywhere else. This is

# A NOTE FROM JENNAE

Thank you so much for reading Love Set Apart.  If you enjoyed this story and have a minute to spare, I would really appreciate a short review on the page or site where you bought the book. Your help in spreading the word is greatly appreciated. Reviews from readers like you make a huge difference in helping new readers find stories similar to Love Set Apart.

If you'd like to know when my next book comes out and want to receive occasional updates from me, then you can sign up for my newsletter here: https://www.subscribepage.com/w4j6s3

# ALSO BY JENNAE VALE

## THE THISTLE & HIVE SERIES

A Bridge Through Time

A Thistle Beyond Time

Separated By Time

A Matter of Time

A Turn In Time

All In Good Time

A Long Forgotten Time

Awakened By Time

Saved By Time

In Time For Edna

A Thistle & Hive Christmas

## THE MACKALLS OF DUNNET HEAD

Her Trusted Highlander

Her Noble Highlander

Her Mysterious Highlander

## THE DELIGHT SERIES

Ross - Prequel

Wanted

Watched

Wounded

Christmas In Delight


THE GREEN SKY SERIES

The Dagger - Prequel

Green Sky At Night

The Golden Hook


EDNA'S WORLD SERIES

Love Set Apart


OTHER BOOKS BY JENNAE

A Highlander In Vegas

# About the Author

Jennae Vale is a best selling author of romance with a touch of magic. As a history buff from an early age, Jennae often found herself day-dreaming in history class and wondering what it would be like to live in the places and time periods she was learning about. Writing time travel romance has given her an opportunity to take those daydreams and turn them into stories to share with readers everywhere.

Originally from the Boston area, Jennae now lives in the San Francisco Bay area, where some of her characters also reside. When Jennae isn't writing, she enjoys spending time with her family and her pets, and daydreaming, of course.

www.jennaevaleauthor.com